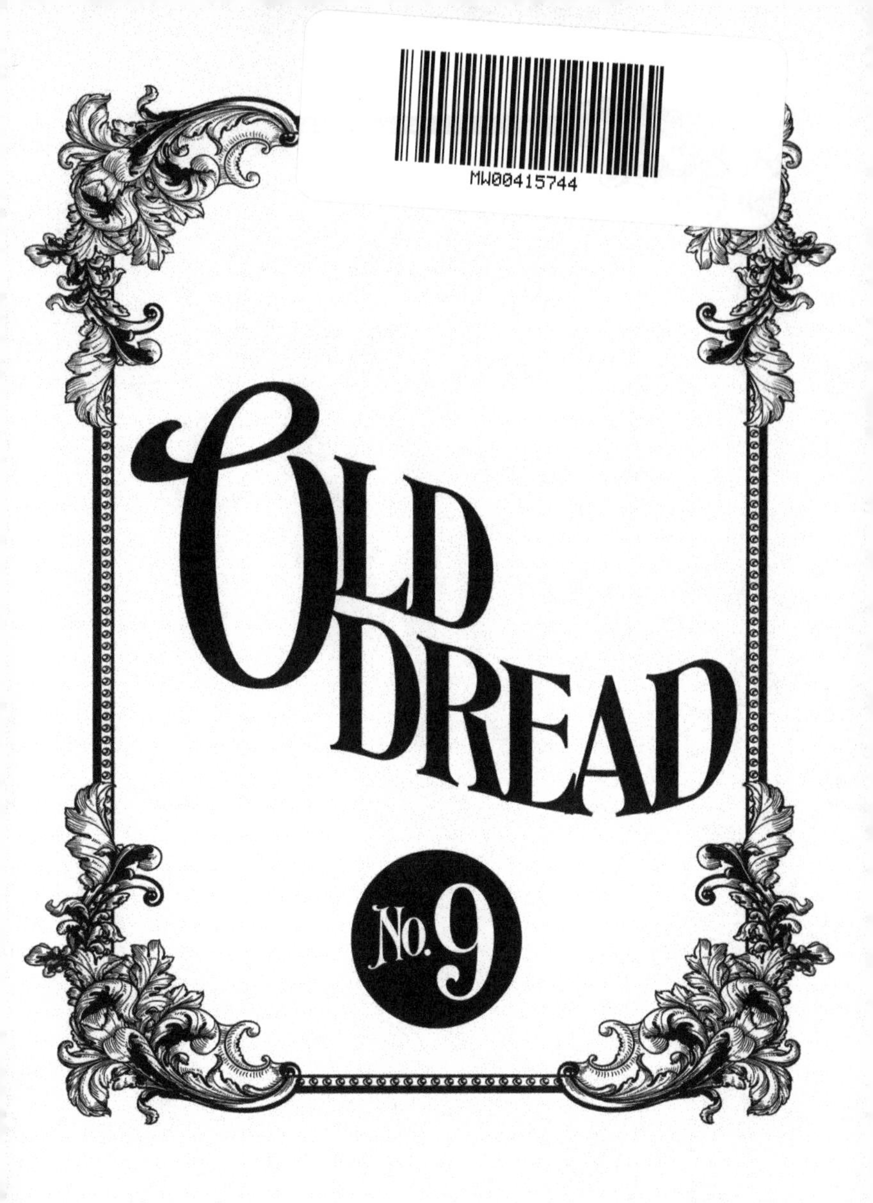

KEN WINKLER

CONTENTS

Cover artwork and formatting by Christian Francis.

Encyclopocalypse Publications
www.encyclopocalypse.com

ACKNOWLEDGMENTS

First and foremost, I'd like to thank my constant champion, Aline Winkler, whose encouragement exceeds reason. My eternal gratitude goes to Ben Meares, who played a role in shaping some of the stories in this collection. Christian Francis, my gifted friend across the pond, you're largely to blame for this monstrosity.

It takes a village (and a little Hell) to raise a book, and this one's no different. Mark Alan Miller, maverick publisher, author, and filmmaker, thank you for allowing me to join the Encyclopocalypse family. To my family and friends, thank you, thank you, and thank you. You dragged me out of the house, you plied me with drinks, you pulled me out of myself, and always when I needed it most.

This is for all of you.

TREASURES

Children of the inner realm
Stand outside the real
Seeking a way in without drawing attention
To themselves, to the secret world they inhabit
Until the time comes
When they must go willingly into the gears
Into the grays
Into the center of the crowd
Ablaze
Trailing colors and scents of faraway lands
Holding fragile treasures in their hands
And there, among countless rows of weary, distrustful eyes
They must learn to say:
Here is my art
Here is my secret
Here is my soul
Name your price

MR. BONES

BETWEEN ANNUAL PERFORMANCES, Mr. Bones counted his mirthless days by the coming and going of a rectangular outline of light through the supply room door, by the sound of small feet stampeding into the classroom just beyond it, and the slippery giggles of restless children taking their seats. Sometimes the door would open at unexpected intervals and the light would blind him, as Mr. Gilford, the custodian, mumbled to himself while reaching for the bag of absorbent shavings he used to soak up the occasional lost lunch of a feverish child.

But today the door would open and Mr. Bones would make an appearance. Even after forty years, with the memories of his former life falling away like brittle leaves, replaced only by an ever-present, pressing sense of *now,* the edge of anticipation hadn't dulled.

Mrs. Atwood's voice rose above the din as she addressed the class. "Quiet, please. Quiet. Charles, turn around and pay attention. Yes, I'm talking to you, mister."

Soon the room settled, and Mr. Bones waited for his cue.

"Thank you. Okay, I want all of you too look at the backs of your hands. Now, using your other hand, I want you to feel your fingers. Squeeze them a little, feel each little digit. Now feel the hard ridges on top your hands." Some of the children laughed. "Good job. Who can tell me what those brittle things are in there?"

"Bones," came a girl's diminutive reply.

"What are they?" Mrs. Atwood said, louder.

"Bo-ones," the children replied.

They seemed less than excited, but just wait, Mr. Bones thought.

"That's right. Here's a tougher question: how many bones do we have in our whole bodies? Anyone. Take a guess."

"Uh, like a hundred," someone offered.

"That's close. Anyone else?"

"A thousand million," a boy said. A swell of raucous debate followed.

"Quiet, please. Thank you. That's too many, Charles."

I know, Mr. Bones thought, but Mrs. Atwood supplied the answer.

"All of us were born with about three hundred, but when we grow up, we end up with two hundred and six."

That always got them to settle and listen.

"Can anyone tell me why we seem to lose some of our bones?"

Again, total silence, broken only by a sniffle or a cough.

"When our teeth fall out," Charles said.

Good one, kid. Mr. Bones liked the spirit in this little fellow.

"Not quite. Our teeth aren't the same as bones. Bones are flexible, and they can heal themselves if they're broken. It was a trick question, because as we grow up, some of our bones fuse together, kind of like when we glue popsicle sticks together. And to help us understand why, today we have a special visitor. He travelled all the way from Ohio to be with us."

Mr. Bones, a true Ohioan—born, raised, and now dead—

grinned, showing two rows of long white teeth that, as the children now knew, were different than bones. The sound of Mrs. Atwood's approaching steps got him grinning wider, as if such a thing were possible, then the door handle turned, and that rectangular outline of light widened, the increasing illumination brighter than Heaven, brighter than sun. Mrs. Atwood's slender silhouette divided the light. The wheels connected to his base squeaked as she rolled him into the room and placed him front and center. Then the world came into view, one shadowy shape at a time, until he found himself staring at a roomful of second-graders.

"Cool," a chubby boy with dense, dark hair said.

Mr. Bones recognized the voice as belonging to Charles, the kid with the excitable imagination. And just look at all the others, seemingly assembled from every country and culture around the world. Much had changed in the last forty years. Most of the children smiled, though some seemed withdrawn, and one or two looked at him as though the Grim Reaper had arrived that morning with disheartening news.

"Class, say hello to Mr. Bones," Mrs. Atwood said.

They replied in clumsy unison, then laughed at the silliness of it all.

And hello to you, he answered, though he knew his greeting went unheard. Nothing delighted him more than showing off his collection to the children, to see the look of astonishment in their eyes, even if his thumb had fallen off long ago, its two phalanges later replaced with plaster replicas, or that someone had put plastic discs between each vertebra of his spine, and connected his ribs to his sternum using that same dull, yellowish plastic. Not a flattering addition. Still, he felt proud that all but two of his bones were original, and that sudden heart failure had taken him instead of some horrible, disfiguring accident.

"I'll have you know that Mr. Bones is a real human skeleton," Mrs. Atwood said.

"He was a person?" a freckled girl asked.

"Yes, he was."

Another girl with two pink butterfly clips in her hair raised her hand.

"Yes, Denise?"

"What happened to him?"

"We don't really know. He came to us a long time ago, long before I was even a teacher; in fact, probably when I was the same age as you are now."

Mysteries within mysteries bloomed behind the girl's eyes.

"Maybe he was bored inside his coffin, and then one day he climbed out and said, 'Hey, it's a nice day. I should go visit some people,'" Charles said.

The children exploded with laughter.

"Charles Hutchins, what on earth did you have for breakfast this morning?" Mrs. Atwood asked, earning another round of laughs.

"Pancakes," he said, without a hint of irony.

Mr. Bones liked this unexpected turn of events. Never before had the subject of his former life become a topic of discussion, and although he'd forgotten much, he wished he could tell them his life had been a rich one; that he'd worked hard to save enough money to buy the feed store his father had taken him to when they still owned the farm, that he'd fallen in love with Judith, a widowed customer who found his easy manner a good fit for her wily nature, and that they'd rebuilt the business after losing it to a fire. He wished he could tell them about his daughter, Michelle, and how much he'd enjoyed reading to her at bedtime. How, in quicker than a blink, she'd grown into a young woman. He also wished he could tell them to hold each day precious. But since he couldn't speak, he had to say it all with a metaphor—his bones.

Mrs. Atwood went on to explain that, without a skeleton, each of them would wilt like pieces of wet laundry hung over a line, that their bones fused together because their growing bodies needed the additional support, and that by age thirty, their bones would become their hardest. She then spun Mr. Bones around and told them that the little thing curling inward below his spine was called a coccyx—a tail, in essence—and that each of them had one. They reached around and checked to see if what she said was true. And then the fun ended.

"Okay everyone, say goodbye to Mr. Bones."

"Ah, can't he stay?" Charles asked.

The kids all whined in support of this idea, then fed off one another's outrage over the injustice of his imprisonment in the closet. Could it be true? Did they really want him to stay?

"Okay, okay. Settle down. We'll put Mr. Bones in the back corner for a while, but do not touch him or play with him. That means you, Charles. He's very delicate, and we can't afford to replace him."

Mrs. Atwood wheeled Mr. Bones to the back of the class, right next to Charles, which also gave him a view of the neighborhood outside the window, and he wept inwardly at seeing so much life moving around out there—the cars, all new and unfamiliar, the clouds drifting by like great white castles, the yellows and golds of fall, tumbling off the trees and clattering over the sidewalks and streets, beckoning winter to come out and play. Each day thereafter, Charles would approach Mr. Bones at the beginning of class, say good morning, and pretend to shake his hand before sitting down. And that's when Mr. Bones' troubles began.

"I'm afraid we have to remove it," the sallow man in a hunter green suit said.

With some difficulty, Mr. Bones recognized him as Mr.

Merrick, the principle. My, how he'd aged! They both stared up at him—Mr. Merrick, with a kind of stern resignation etched deep into his long features, and Mrs. Atwood, who looked disgusted by the whole affair.

"Charles was just expressing his creativity. He's gifted, and his parents need to understand that," she said.

"Our job is to teach these children, not to test their parents' patience."

"I disagree. I think they need to be challenged, parents and children."

"Claire, when a child goes around telling everyone his best friend is a skeleton, it raises troubling questions. You understand. And his folks weren't the only ones who complained. Several called me after the last open house and said it was inappropriate—morbid, even—to have such a thing staring over their children's shoulders in class. Another suggested that we put clothes on it."

"That's ridiculous," she said. "The kids adore him."

"This isn't a case of majority rule. I'm sorry, but it goes. Good afternoon," he said, turning toward the door.

"I tried, but it looks like this is goodbye, Mr. Bones."

She turned off the light before departing, leaving him to ponder his fate as a bank of dense cloud slid over the sky, sealing him in premature nightfall. However, he didn't find rest that evening. He never rested, and the following day before class, Mr. Gilford wheeled him out of the classroom, down the hallway, and into a storage room deeper and darker than the one he'd previously occupied.

The door slammed shut with echoing authority.

If Mr. Bones could explain the feeling of eternity to someone, he'd say it's the exponential dividing of seconds into ever-widening gaps of time that became so vast, so incalculable, that all one could do is stare right down the middle of a moment, and wait; therefore, he didn't how much time had passed when the door reopened, only that Mr. Gilford hadn't opened it. Rather, the silhouettes of two young men stood in the doorway, each staring into the murk.

"There it is," the taller one said, pointing.

The light outside the storage room seemed bright enough to bleach onyx, but it soon mellowed to a bluish hue. A cold winter's day. The workers, each dressed in gray coveralls, dropped a pine box the size of a casket onto the floor and opened the lid. It contained countless pieces of colored packing foam. Just as Mr. Bones recognized their intentions, the shorter worker threw a clear sheet of plastic over him, the effect blurring the world, like a camera's lens losing focus. Then the two amateur undertakers tilted him backwards. The ceiling's acoustical tiles came into view, presenting a barrier between this world and the next, then down he went, into the box.

"Be careful," the one in charge said.

"Yep."

They placed him face-up in a soft bedding of foam, then poured more over him, covering his legs, chest, and face, the combination of plastic and packing material arousing in the hollow chamber of his skull a latent fear of suffocation. Not unlike a burial, he thought, except they were doing it all wrong. He believed he needed the sanctity of earth to see the deed done right, or a good, cleansing fire to scorch his bones to ash. He needed someone to sprinkle his remains into a lake or river, his material essence flowing into low-lying fields, feeding dormant seeds and old growth trees, his spirit reconstituted in every pattern of leaf. Oh, to dance in the breeze, present only to the bees and the sun and changing of seasons.

He needed a burial rite, or a group of mourners all dressed in black, each approaching his casket and wishing him well on his journey, not two young workers blithely sealing him up with his angst. No, he would not find peace this day. And what would happen to the rest of his memories over time? Would they continue to fade like old lessons erased from a chalkboard? And what would remain, a vague impression of self, a faulty awareness of space and time, complicated by an inability to impose his will upon either?

He remembered that some spiritual teachings called for embracing the present, and only then could one know true peace. What a basket of road apples! He'd pretty much achieved that dubious state of divine presentness, meditating like a monk next to a broom inside the closet for years. He'd much rather have his flesh returned to him, and his family, along with his desires and will, his hopes and fears, and his mortal sense of time, which had lent a wondrous urgency to life. Yes, dwelling on the past had been a problem while living, and fretting about the future had haunted him more often than he cared to recall, but no fancy trick of the mind could ever replace the joy of having seen his daughter alight upon some immense discovery, like the time a grasshopper landed on her bare knee. She didn't jump. She didn't shriek. She sat still and watched in wonder, remarking that its long legs accounted for its ability to jump great distances. He remembered her look of shock when it leapt from her knee and flapped away on a pair of flickering, clicking wings, or the time... or the time...

He knew countless other jewels of experience lay somewhere in the storehouse of memory, but the deeper he looked, the darker it appeared.

The ground beneath him rumbled, then it seemed to slide beneath him. A metal door slid shut, and the sound of a diesel engine roared to life. He was on the road, rattling around in his box, staring wide-eyed into a false oblivion, as the sound of bluegrass music jangled hollow and thin through the truck's cab. Well, at least he was moving through space and time, and maybe to somewhere exciting—maybe back home, to... Ohio, was it? He thought about the surrogate family he'd left behind in Mrs. Atwood's classroom. Had that been his life? Was his name really Mr. Bones? It all seemed like a collage of overlapping impressions and half-truths.

The cycle of motion, stillness, the opening and closing of doors, and strangers' voices repeated several times, until he felt himself come to rest in a large, open space, given the echo his box produced when they dropped it on the floor. Moment opened to moment, like two mirrors facing each other—no beginning or end, just the next, and the next, and the next. Lacking the ability to scream, he settled his raging thoughts and tried to focus on a single image. He saw a red tractor rusting away inside of an old barn.

It would have to do.

A roomful of young people seated in ascending rows of chairs looked at something over Mr. Bones' shoulder—something glowing, changing colors, like slides cycling through a projector. Some in the audience jotted notes with pen and paper, while others tapped on devices he didn't recognize, as though typing, the screens opened before them illuminating their faces. Mr. Bones realized he now occupied a university lecture hall. Then his hearing returned, but where had it gone? The tractor took it. No, that didn't seem right.

"...to help you identify the leading causes of Greenstick fractures. Someday, if some of you achieve that glorious status of orthopedic specialist, a frantic parent will step into your office holding a crying child, unaware that a fracture had even occurred. And believe me when I tell you that your first job will not be to evaluate the patient, but to calm the parent."

As the lecture continued, only one person took keen interest in him. This young man appeared strait-laced and attentive, his books and notes well-organized on his desk. Then something amazing happened. The young man smiled at him.

I'm here! I see you! My name is... my name is Mr. Bones, I think.

As the days came and went, he regained a more measurable sense of time, and through a series of regular gatherings, the students became his new family, along with the professor, whom he only ever glimpsed now and then. The days turned into weeks, months, and then years, and the faces he saw changed, but all the students, whether juniors or seniors, whether bored or interested, addressed him by his new name—Henry, or good old Hank, on occasion. And whenever the professor wheeled him forward to illustrate a point, Mr. Bones would feel like a useful contributor, providing calcified substance to more abstract concepts. Bones, he learned, were rigid organs that stored minerals and produced red and white blood cells. Bones protected the heart and brain, those two most precious of human organs.

After twenty years of the same routine, while assuming his new identity with no little stubbornness, he saw the return of student who'd smiled at him an age ago. Now well-dressed and with streaks of gray in his hair, he entered the lecture hall alongside the professor, whose old age brought Mr. Bones up to date with the passage of time.

"I can't believe he's still here," the former student said, his eyes taking in every detail. "You sure you can part with him?"

"Oh, I think so. Hank and I had a good run together, and I like the idea of him spooking your patients a little."

"They'll love him. Believe me."

Not long after, they put Mr. Bones in another box, and although his journey in darkness lasted only two days, it felt more like forever and a day. By the time the smiling student—now a doctor, Mr. Bones learned—positioned him in the small exam room, providing him a view of a cabinet, a door, and an exam table, his memory had become a white flag whipping in the wind. Who was he? But the days resumed with regularity, and then he remembered. He was Hank, Hank the skeleton. He'd always been a skeleton, and all of the people entering the room, sitting down, and holding out their arms to have their blood pressure taken were patients. Some of them stared at Mr. Bones with a kind of wariness, as though his appearance portended some dreadful, unavoidable outcome.

Every so often a child accompanied by an adult would enter, and he or she would dart to Mr. Bones and flick his ribs or wiggle his fingers, all to the dismay of the adults. Whenever this happened, a phantom longing would arise within him, along with the fleeting image of a cute little girl he'd once known very well, but she could have been one of the patients. Still, it seemed vital that he snatch that memory the next time it flitted by, like a grasshopper disappearing into the brush.

The years came and went, and when some of Dr. Richmond's more curious patients asked, he would tell them the story of how Hank came into his possession, and why he felt sentimental about the old fellow. Mr. Bones, hearing this story told over and over again, took it as gospel. And just before the last of his old memories faded away, the nurse led a heavy-set man with a thick matt of salt and pepper hair into the exam room, and who, with a half-formed smile and baleful look in his eyes, took a seat on the table.

"How are you today, Mr. Hutchins?" she asked.

Hello, Mr. Hutchins, Mr. Bones said. He said hello to all of the patients, always hoping they might reply.

"I don't feel a day over sixty-five," he said.

Despite the man's droll sense of humor, Mr. Bones noticed something odd in the exchange. Roiling beneath the surface of pleasantries lurked an awkward tension neither seemed willing to confront. As the nurse strapped a band around his arm and took his blood pressure, Mr. Hutchins's eyes drifted toward Mr. Bones, and for a moment Mr. Bones believed the man could see him; or rather, that he could see the soul behind the skull.

"You ready for the holidays?" the nurse said, making conversation.

"If you mean fighting the traffic and the crowds, and doing all of my shopping at the last minute, then yes."

"Isn't that how it always goes? Every year I swear that I won't stay up till midnight wrapping presents, but I always end up doing it." She removed the band from his arm then took his temperature. "Normal. The doctor will be in shortly."

"Okay. Thanks."

During the conversation, Mr. Hutchins never took his eyes off Mr. Bones, and even after the nurse the left the room, he continued to stare. A moment later, Dr. Richmond stepped in, carrying several files under his arm.

"Good afternoon, I'm Dr. Richmond."

"Good to meet you," Mr. Hutchins said, shaking the doctor's hand.

"I want you to know that I spent a considerable amount of time going over your records, and that I've spoken with Dr. Talbot."

Mr. Hutchins seemed calm as he listened and nodded, but his hands told a different story, the tension in them unmistakable, as he gripped the edge of the table.

"Forgive me for prying, but what's your support structure like at home?"

Mr. Hutchins smiled. "You can just tell me. I won't hold it against you."

Dr. Richmond gathered his thoughts, and said, "I'm afraid I have to agree with the prognosis. Even with aggressive treatment—radiation therapy, bone marrow transplant—the cancer will continue to spread at an alarming rate. You could fight it, and I encourage all my patients to fight for each day, but sometimes, and I don't like doing this, I have to tell them to make whatever peace they need to make, and to prepare themselves as they transition—"

"Yes. I understand. I... understand." Mr. Hutchins let loose a heavy sigh. "Sorry. After you've heard the same story several times, you start to get the idea of how it's going to end. Anyway, that's strike three, and I believe I'm out." He got up from the table and stepped toward Mr. Bones.

"That's Hank," the doctor said. "He helps out around here."

"Hank, huh? Maybe I could borrow some of his bones. What do you say, Hank?"

Something about this man's sense of humor struck a resounding chord within Mr. Bones. *Who was he?*

"There are still some practical things you can do... with a healthy diet, exercise..."

"Okay, now you're really killing me," Mr. Hutchins said, laughing.

"Do you have anyone—family, friends—who can help you through it?"

"Yes and no. I'm divorced. I have a son. He's a great kid, stubborn like his dad, but we haven't spoken in a while."

"Now's the time, Mr. Hutchins."

"I believe you're right," he answered, as though some rusted lock had clicked open in his mind.

Time was everything, Mr. Bones thought. It was everything because that's all anyone ever had, and the punishment for forgetting this simple rule was a lifetime of waiting, dreaming, and forgetting. He'd become the world's leading expert on the subject. But how? Had he once been alive? Yes, he had, he realized with sudden amazement.

"If there's anything else I can do for you, please let me know. Melinda will get you out of here and on with your day."

"Thanks, Doc," he said. "Happy holidays."

When the door closed, Mr. Hutchins put his hands on his waist and stared at the ceiling, though it appeared to Mr. Bones that he was staring at something beyond the ceiling.

"Now's the time. There is no time," Mr. Hutchins whispered to himself. He turned his gaze back toward Mr. Bones, then approached him with his hand extended. "Put her there, Hank," he said, placing Mr. Bones' hand into his own. But as he looked down, something in his expression changed. Curiosity gave way to disbelief, then to shock. "It couldn't be," he said, inspecting Mr. Bones' plaster thumb. "Mr. Bones, is that you? It's me, Charles. Charles Hutchins."

The memories crashed over Mr. Bones like a massive wave, tumbling him to and fro, up and down, into a maelstrom of memory. In the disorienting madness of it all, he saw the university lecture hall, the darkness of concealment inside the pine box, then the second-grade classroom—Mrs. Atwood's classroom. Yes, of course! And the man before him was Charles, the boy with the fierce wit who'd made everyone laugh. Then he found himself inside the supply closet, the sour expression on Mr. Gilford's face as he reached for the absorbent shavings a welcome sight. Further back he went, all the way to the mysterious time before that time. He lay in a room filled with greenish light. Men in hospital scrubs surrounded him, their mouths hidden behind surgical masks. One of them leaned over and lifted a scalpel toward his chest. Then came a flash of light. He now stood in his driveway clutching his chest, unable to untwist the unbearable pain in his heart. He dropped to his knees as a panicked woman ran toward him. Not just any woman, but his wife. Back further still. He found himself fixing a red tractor inside the barn, *his* barn. Then he was opening a present a young girl had given him. That girl was his daughter, Michelle. Oh, you sweet, sweet child. Of course, he was surprised, and he needed that new tie, after all. Judith sat nearby, her warm hand touching his. He suddenly knew everything about his former life. His name had been Oliver Wilks, and in the remembering, he became acutely aware that some horrible error had left him trapped inside his own skeleton.

"You've been working too long," Charles said. "I tell you what. We'll both take a long vacation. How does that sound?"

Yes, Mr. Bones thought. *Please.* I can't stay here one moment longer.

"May you rest in peace, Mr. Bones," he said.

And for the first time in an age, Mr. Bones did just that.

ALL THE PRETTY SKULLS

Skulls, everywhere!
In the supermarket, surveying the produce
Peering into the freezer, the cold air intimating
The chill of the grave
Skulls at the park, at the pool, at the beach
Nodding off in offices on spindles of vertebrae
Skulls turning to meet other skulls
Skulls blowing out birthday candles
Blowing kisses
Blowing steam on a pair of glasses
Bowing in prayer
Bowing in shame
Bending down to smell the roses
Turning toward passing skulls they find attractive
Or gazing toward a canopy of stars
Looking, always looking
Inward, outward; past and future
For answers
Their brains like alien organisms
At odds with their bodies, and better sense

And so they look into books, into matters
Into the nature of matter itself
Skulls with knowledge of skulls
Skulls thudding on desks in frustration
Skulls with clashing ideas
Skulls clashing with truncheons
With bullets and bombs
Skulls on the battlefield not as pretty
As the skull brushing its silken hair
Before a mirror, seeing itself hidden there
Skulls with gods inside them, or ghosts
And often too many delusions
Skulls risen to kings and queens, crowned
And kept down in the dark, in the catacombs
All grinning along darkened tunnels
Made equal at last
For there is one thing upon which all skulls agree:
That in time they'll overthrow the tyranny of flesh
And the confused directives from central command
And manifest, from one to the last, their true identities

THE LEAF TRADERS

They trade their gold for time
The maples in this town
Bartering in fall, begging in winter
When all their leaves turn brown

But no one seems to want
The bounty left aground
Brushed away, burned to ash
Like so much squandered cash

And yet among these riches
With seasons few to cling
The old and gray will kick their way
Trading in joy for one more spring

OR SO I'M TOLD

I'm too old
To dress all in black
Or get more tattoos
Or sprout bat wings
To attract the night things

I'm too old
For the absence of color
They say it doesn't fit
A man fit for salmon
Or teal
Or the colors of the real

"But the night things!
How will they find me?"

"Don't worry," they say.
"They'll find you in the diner,
Before six o'clock,

On the golf course,
Or reading in bed,
And will know
You're already dead."

DAY & NIGHT

The ward got away—
escaped the sheets and mystery
to the madness of the day

But nighttime always comes—
it opens wide and swallows whole
its weary, errant son

BEYOND THE WALL

"There's another world through here," the girl with horns said to Elroy.

She placed her hands on either side of a bright, paper-thin fissure in the stone wall, which was ancient and tall, and shrouded in brown, brittle ivy. It seemed to stretch to infinity in both directions, though no one knew who'd taken the trouble to build it. Above the wall, deep blue twilight; higher still, vast constellations.

Elroy drew close to his companion, who stood tall, pale, and bird-bone thin. She had long, silken white hair. He loved her horns, the way they curled upwards in graceful arcs. Never mind they lacked uniformity in shape. If anything, this flaw made her more interesting, more wonderful. A single line of light projecting through the fissure divided her eye, which was black as oil and filled with dreams, and whenever she looked skyward, he could see the stars reflected in them. It was all too much for a man who'd never experienced reciprocated love from someone far more attractive than himself.

"Look for yourself," she said, smiling, then stepping aside.

Elroy approached, pulled away some of the ivy as though

parting curtains, and peered through the crack. It wasn't a single line of white light, as he'd first suspected; rather, it opened to a prism of sorts, and the closer he leaned in, the more he saw. A kind of depth presented itself. Each side of the fissure appeared blurred, as though made of ephemeral magic, and the impressionistic shapes it contained moved like spirits.

"Keep looking. You'll see it," she said, her voice confident.

He tilted his head side-to-side, leaned in closer, and the image came into sharp focus. Beyond the wall, he saw a grocery store aisle, with brightly colored cereal boxes lining shelves. Then a woman in tight-fitting gym clothes came into view, pushing a shopping cart filled with enough food to feed a village. Her two young boys raced ahead of her and pointed toward the box of cereal they wanted. The mother, unmoved by their pleas, removed the box and read the description of ingredients on the side, then placed it back on the shelf. An argument ensued, but no sound accompanied it.

"Isn't it wonderful?" she asked, placing her hands on his shoulders. Her long, cool fingers transported him to secret wells of desire, and he found himself unable to respond. "There's another one farther down the wall. It's a place where people sit and drink from little white cups. And they have these devices. They're mirrors, I think, because they stare into them all the time. And the people there are all so beautiful. They look like you. It's where you came from, isn't it?"

Despite feeling flattered, he wouldn't give up his secrets. "I'd never looked through the wall before today. Anyway, it's much more beautiful here."

The latter part was true. He'd awoken one day beside a black pond, its surface serene as glass, and just beneath the surface, a graceful, bioluminescent form appeared, curling upwards and floating there, regarding him with a pair of luminous eyes that signaled amusement. It then darted downward, leaving ripples on the pond's surface that diminished along the shore. Leafless trees with contorted arms reached across the pond, as if to delve into its depths. The air was cool and earth-tinged, but not cold. It was twilight then, as it was now, and always was, and the sky had been alive with black-winged creatures that screeched and swooped toward ground level, gathering green fireflies into the folds of their wings, and devouring them. Far off in the woods he heard music—a dissonant, tumbling tune—produced by instruments he couldn't name. The lead melody seemed to his delighted ears a bittersweet threnody, and hearing it, tears overcame him. At last, he'd found his true home.

"We must find a way through," she said.

"Let's go swimming instead."

"We did that yesterday."

"But today we might find something else, maybe a new channel."

They'd spent the last several days exploring the underwater caverns that intersected with the other ponds throughout the forest, and since they could breathe underwater, exploration had been a joy. The rocks below the water emitted a soft white light, and the creature he'd seen the day of his arrival reappeared, beckoning them both deeper. More creatures awaited in the depths, many more, in a cavern deep below the surface. Drifting through the throng of radiant beings, Elroy and his companion found themselves amidst a ritual, with two of the creatures intertwined in a corkscrew of motion. They spun faster as their lips met, and then the two fused into a single being far more beautiful than its former halves, as the others emitted lilting tones of celebration.

The creatures urged Elroy and his companion to do the same. They embraced and attempted to circle one another in the same fashion, but when they kissed, nothing happened. Still, it had been transcendent for Elroy, and his companion seemed equally spellbound. The creatures, however, had been frightened by their inability to merge into one, and fled.

That was before she'd become consumed with the wall.

"I can't imagine how wonderful it must be—all those things to taste, all the colors, the clothing they wear, the things they have. They seem to have everything, don't they?" she asked.

"But do any of them look happy?"

"What do you mean?"

"You weren't looking very carefully," he said, walking away, but she didn't follow. Turning back, he saw a look of doubt cross her features. She leaned toward the fissure with renewed interest.

She grew despondent after the experience at the wall. They no longer made love, though not by his choice, and he'd often find her sitting by the wall, staring through the fissure for hours, engrossed in the goings-on behind it.

"Come away from there," he said. "You wouldn't like people spying on you all the time."

"They can't see me," she said, distracted. "At first, I thought they all looked the same, but they're all so different from one another. Why do you think they eat all the time?"

"They're bored."

"I don't think they're bored. It looks like they're thinking—all the time thinking. To create and live in a world like that, they must have incredible minds."

He stopped himself from offering any contradictory evidence. He didn't want to hurt her feelings. "I hear there's an elevation party happening on the bluffs. You feel like flying? The clouds are perfect tonight."

"You go ahead," she replied, leaning closer to the wall.

. . .

That night, drunk and drifting just over the edge of the bluffs with the other partygoers, whose arms and legs were festooned with long ribbons, and whose jeweled goblets of wine sloshed around in their careless hands, he didn't reach the same level of euphoria he'd experienced before. All he could think about was her, sitting alone down there alone and staring at a world she'd come to believe was better than this one.

"To the river!" someone cried out.

"To the river," several others echoed, as they twirled through the mist and shot downward.

He didn't follow, though. He didn't want to be that far away from her tonight.

Later, lying beside her—the stars softly chiming in his ears, the light breeze lifting fine strands of her hair—he held her closer than ever. Behind her closed lids lay a world unto itself; one that he could never enter, nor inhabit. Her eyelids fluttered open, and suddenly he was alive again—he existed.

She rolled over to face him and caressed his cheek. "Do you think they're all unhappy?" she asked.

"Yes," he said, thinking of the past—his job, the bills, disappointing people, being disappointed by them, and just the overall pressure of living. He remembered his phobias and fears, the mad pursuit of material success that, once attained, would somehow validate him in the eyes of others. His mood darkened, and he hoped more than anything that he'd never wake up in that other world again. Eventually sleep took him, and his dreams were wonderful, because they resembled the place he now resided.

"You have to see this. Hurry," she called up to him.

Elroy stood high in a tree, reaching toward a rare fruit known to produce fantastic hallucinations.

"Hurry, before they go away."

The fuzzy-skinned fruit dangled just beyond reach, but he continued straining for it.

"It will be there when you get back. Just hurry."

No sooner than his feet touched the ground did she snatch his hand and drag him toward the wall. *The wall, the wall.* He was tired of the wall.

"Look," she said, pulling him close.

"What am I supposed to see?"

"The girls. You see the three girls?"

Through the fissure he saw an outdoor restaurant patio by the beach. It was summer, and each table was full. At the table nearest him sat three teenage girls in bathing suits, their heads lowered, as they sipped iced juice drinks through bright red straws, but their devious eyes strayed toward someone else at the next table. One of them whispered, then the girls erupted with laughter.

"They're happy, aren't they?" she asked.

"Yes, you've found a group of people enjoying themselves," came Elroy's reluctant reply.

"So, it's true, then. I knew it! I always knew it."

"Look again," he said, urging her forward. They looked through the wall together.

It seemed the source of the girls' dubious joy was a heavy-set girl of similar age, who sat at the next table next to them with her back turned, unaware she'd become an object of ridicule. The prettiest of the laughing girls threw a piece of ice at the back of her head. The victim turned, singling out the culprit, but the three girls feigned innocence, then burst into laughter when their victim looked away.

"Why does it make them happy, treating her that way?"

"They think they're prettier than the other one."

"Shouldn't they love her, regardless?"

"They don't think in terms of love."

"How do you know that?"

"You'll just have to take my word," he said, uninterested in pursuing the topic further.

Elroy's companion remained unconvinced, however, and seemed determined to prove him wrong. And so, they walked along the wall, stopping here and there whenever a crack appeared. The world beyond the wall only became more vicious and inhumane. They saw a schoolyard fight, then flinched at the sight of someone getting stabbed outside a liquor store. They witnessed two men holding a woman down while a third ripped off pants. The perpetrators, whose pants hung around their ankles, cheered each other on, as the woman, who appeared drugged, attempted to defend herself. They saw a little girl covered in dust and blood sitting on the ground and crying, as all around her a bombed-out city burned. Each twisted menagerie was bathed in daylight, as though the people who'd committed these atrocities took pride in their misdeeds, and *wanted* others to see them. They saw desperation and madness, and people killing others for gain, revenge, or perhaps the plain pleasure of seeing life dwindle from a pair of panicked eyes. Some areas of the wall contained gaps wide enough to walk through, and these areas contained the greatest of human horrors.

Elroy described in detail what they'd witnessed, thus providing his companion a speed-course education of life in the real world. It left her in tears, but he didn't take pleasure in it. He'd broken her fantasy, and it broke his heart for having done it.

"You're one of them, aren't you?" she said, the fear in her voice unmistakable.

"Not anymore," he said, and he meant it.

"You wouldn't hurt me?"

"Never. I would never hurt you." And when they embraced, he no longer felt the subtle resistance he'd come to notice over the last few days.

"Promise me you'll never go back."

"That's an easy promise to make."

"I need you to say it."

"As long as I'm alive and have a choice, I'll never go back."

When Elroy woke the next day, he felt something unusual on his forehead: a light pressure of sorts arising from two points, and when he touched them a wave of relief swept over him. Just above his forehead sprouted two baby horns, the skin around each breached area tender. He wondered if the fruit he'd plucked and eaten had somehow instigated this transformation, before relegating it to natural phenomena. Whether by way of something eaten or drunk, whether the growth of his horns resulted from his time there, or perhaps his time with *her*, it seemed to indicate he'd achieved the status of permanent resident, a naturalized inhabitant of the "other side." Would his connection to this world deepen over time? Would his eyes turn black like hers, and if they did, what would he see?

As it stood, he'd only just begun to explore the landscape. He knew of a city not far down river, a place called Gondolee, and he knew that cities contained people (or beings, in this case) who often lived at cross-purposes, battling on ambition's chessboard for prestige and prizes; for higher positions within their chosen fields, and, ultimately, for crowns, presidencies, and dictatorships. Would he find cruelty there? Would he ever see another sunrise? Would he come to regret losing contact with his family and friends?

In the end, he felt he belonged in this place—or *to* it, and it him—and hoped they'd understand. With this hope came a vow to endure the consequences of his desire to stay, no matter the magnitude of his guilt for having left them with unanswered questions. He'd stay until the people he knew abandoned all hope for his return. He'd stay until his name ceased to fall from their lips, and the vowels contained in the name "Elroy" no longer formed in their thoughts. He'd stay forever—there, in the dreaming place, where wonder and mystery unfolded at a gentler pace, and where revelation arrived on wings of inspiration, rather than black gales of regret.

He later found his companion swimming in the pond. He watched her awhile, as she divided the dark water in graceful strokes and turns, and when she emerged on the shore, draped in streaming rivulets of water and nothing more, he marveled at the solid persistence of his new home, while taking joy in the realistic, reliable kind of love he'd always hoped to find. She approached with a smile, a miracle made flesh, her skin the scent of fresh fruit, her tongue the taste of the rarest nectar. Yet she possessed her own mind, her own universe of being, and the innocence he mistook for naïveté struck him now as a kind of wisdom. She'd seen the horrors beyond the wall without losing touch with the transcendent. She'd recognized in him a connection to the species responsible, and despite the knowing, despite the danger, and despite possessing a wealth of beauty, which endowed her with a dealer's choice in lovers, she'd elected to remain by his side. She found him beautiful, impossible as it seemed.

The trees around the pond seemed to twist with age and envy, as his companion wrung the water from her long hair. Elroy choked back a breath, then strode toward her and bowed to show off his fledgling horns.

"They're purple. That's a good sign," she said, touching them.

"It is?"

"You have no idea."

. . .

That afternoon they joined their friends—horned, winged, fantastical creatures all, and each alluring in their way—and together they gathered clay and stones from the shores of various ponds and rivers in the area. Some brought along buckets and spades, and they spent the remainder of the day filling the fissures in the wall, thus sealing off the real world for good, and when they finished, they celebrated on the bluffs, then chased after each other into the sky.

The following morning, Elroy walked along the wall inspecting the previous day's work, his head still humming with drink and song, his lips and loins raw from a wine-induced marathon session of lovemaking with his companion, whom he'd left sleeping beside the pond, her curiosity about the wall kissed out of existence. None of them would qualify as masons on the other side, but they'd done a sufficient job of cordoning off the unsavory sights the real world it contained. The clay had already begun to dry and harden in areas, melding seamlessly into the overall architecture. He scratched one such area with a fingernail, which had grown thick, long, and pointed overnight. He held his hands outward, palms facing downward, fingers spread wide. "What do you know about that? Claws."

Claws for digging, claws for scratching, claws for…

He looked up. By a trick of perception, the wall stretched out before him like a stone pathway. Just an illusion, however.

"Huh," he said to no one.

If he wanted to see the big picture—and he wasn't entirely sure that he did—he'd have to climb. Driven as much by the curiosity of his climbing ability as by the sights he might glimpse from the top, he dug into the porous mortar around the stones, and sure enough, his claws held steady. The pointed nails protruding from his toes were thicker and shorter, as though designed to bear a greater load. He dug into the wall with his toenails. They accepted his weight without protest, and so Elroy ascended by digging in, then pulling himself upward. In short time he sweated out the wine he'd drunk the previous night.

It's a fool's mission, he thought, looking back down with renewed sobriety. He'd only climbed twenty feet or so, not high enough to see beyond the canopy of orange and red leaves above, though high enough to put the fear of the fall in him. Of course, he wanted to gain a better sense of the geography he inhabited, but a deeper curiosity—one that he dared not whisper in thought—propelled him higher.

With every upward inch gained, the memory of his former life appeared in greater detail: He'd just been promoted from Quality Assurance Analyst I to Quality Assurance Analyst II, which meant he could afford a payment on a better car, freshen his wardrobe, and get a new tattoo, and wouldn't that impress Jenna? Jenna! Dear God! He'd almost forgotten about her. He'd loved her in secret from across the cubicle aisle for three torturous years, the scent of her hair driving him mad, her voice unstitching his soul at the seams. Whenever she answered the phone, and said, "Benevolife Health Solutions, Jenna speaking, how may I help you?" a little part of him died. What happened to her in his absence? he wondered, climbing higher. Did she miss him? Oh, how he wished she missed him, and wouldn't that teach her a lesson for ignoring him, and not appreciating his charms?

And he hadn't finished helping his mother (widowed for a decade) replace the drafty old windows on her neglected bungalow. He'd meant to do it sooner, but he'd always been just a little too busy—drinking with friends and watching sports, then shouting when his team dropped the ball, or missed the shot, or…

A wave of shame swept over him, as the wind blustered

beneath his feet, carrying with it the sweet aroma of his new home, his true home, where he'd smiled for the first time without a hint of sadness behind it in years. He glanced down.

"Whoa!" The ground seemed to fall away from his feet. He'd achieved dizzying heights; had crested the tops of the trees, in fact, so that it appeared he'd poked his head above a sea of fiery clouds, all stirring and churning, the leaves a billion brittle butterflies rubbing their wings together in the purple glow of not-quite-night.

Muscles shaking with the first signs of failure, Elroy clung halfway between the ground and the top of the wall, above which he discerned the division between twilight and wonder on his side, and daylight and blunder the other. He'd come this high without falling, he reasoned, so why not see the job through? He'd have to hurry, though, because he didn't know if he possessed the stamina to cling there much longer.

He made ready to climb, but as he removed his right hand from the wall, the claw on his index finger tore off and remained wedged in the mortar. The blood flowed quickly from the exposed flesh. He cringed, shouted, then shook his hand, as though to shake away the pain throbbing in time with his elevated heartbeat. He pulled on the nail that had broken off in the wall, with a half-formed notion that he might re-attach it, but it wouldn't budge.

And what about his mail? He had bills that needed paying, and he'd been expecting a new cable TV receiver box to arrive any day now. If the delivery driver left it on his porch, there was a good chance some enterprising porch pirate would snatch it.

He knew he had to hurry.

SNAP! Off came another nail—this one from his left big toe. His stomach fell in advance of his left foot, which dangled midair. He gripped the wall tighter, then moaned as he clambered upward, digging in with greater desperation. His remaining claws seemed to loosen, like rotted teeth in need of pulling. Blood collected around the cuticles, then dripped down the backs of his hands. *My dog! Who's been taking care of Stan?* For all he knew, Stan had died of a lack of food, water, and affection, unaware that his master had abandoned him for better-smelling company. Elroy scrambled upward as best he could, losing more nails in the effort, and growing increasingly aware of not only his former life, but the prospect of a terrible fall from grace should he fail to reach the top. His left foot had been shorn of claws, and so he relied upon his bleeding toes to find small ledges—less than half an inch, in some cases—in the stones for support.

Death seemed close. It breathed in his ear. But no, it was the wind, carrying his companion's voice toward his ears from far below: a disconnected call from a fever dream. She repeated his name, the echoes diminishing in the trees, then trailing off in the opposite direction.

"I'm up here! Help!" he said, but the wind devoured his voice.

The precipice loomed just out of reach, mocking him. He had only to reach another ten inches, but that would require removing his right foot from the wall, and would leave him dangling by two claws—one on his left pinky, the other on his right thumb. He had two choices: make the leap upward, or fall backward, and hope that a branch might break his fall. He chose the former. Employing what little strength remained, Elroy sprung upward with desperation. He got a hand over the edge, then pulled himself toward the top, getting one leg over the other. He straddled the wall, nearly weeping with relief.

"I'm such an idiot," he said, panting and shaking.

Elroy sat high above and *between* two worlds collecting his breath and sanity. He glanced right, toward the magical land from which he'd just climbed. The expanse of forest—its beauty and fecundity, the knocking, chirping sounds it produced—held him spellbound, as did the stars above, and he yearned to return to it once he'd slaked his curiosity, assuming he could climb back down. The trees terminated at the edge of the bluffs, below which ran a wide, dark green river—the same river he and his three-toed friends would often lounge beside while drinking themselves blind. He had difficulty seeing beyond that portion of land, which he first ascribed to a layer of cloud or mist, but that didn't explain the phenomenon in full. It was as though the unexplored areas of wonderland simply didn't exist, or that the artist's brush had run dry before she'd had a chance to finish the masterpiece, as wispy strokes of color swept upward toward gray nothingness, then disappeared into it.

A frightening notion gripped him: was he the maker of this land? Was the expanse of it dependent upon further exploration of areas that, once glimpsed, would forever exist in memory, like a living map? If so, didn't that suggest he had a tremendous responsibility to see it constructed with caution, care and, most of all, love? And what if his mood turned black? Would war ensue? Would famine and disease rush in to fill his lapse in compassion for all things delicate and beautiful? He didn't know, and suspected that by merely asking these questions, he'd already invited doubt into the picture—into his world, more precisely, if the thornier part of the theory had merit.

Another sound and scent stole his attention. He turned his gaze to the left side of wall, and toward the Land of Sorrows; that is, toward his old home. The labyrinth of cities and residential districts far below hummed with millions of engines, buzzing electrical lines, trains and planes, and human cries. The soot and sweat-tinged air that wafted toward him intermingled with the sweeter scents of nirvana to his right, the confluence of these disparate climates mirroring the conflict in his soul. He looked down in despair.

It appeared the real world had crashed into the wall, like a wave of drywall, brick, steel beams, and shingles, and the damaged architecture suggested these structures had poured in from all over the world—orange and lime green favelas stood in riot with brushed steel office buildings, French villas butted heads with Russian onion domes. Countless other combinations he couldn't describe became apparent in the twisted milieu, which rose and fell in great ripples, as though fluid, and receded into the hazy distance. And the cruelty and horrors Elroy and his companion had witnessed from the other side continued in earnest. Didn't the people below know they stood within a mental leap of a wondrous place, a place they'd seen in their gentlest summer snoozes? Perhaps they did, and turned their anger toward each other for having caught a glimpse and been kept out. Elroy shuddered to think that his life awaited him down there, among the mazes and traps, the random acts of violence.

He walked along the top of the wall, arms outstretched for balance. For all its injustices, the Land of Sorrows also contained a lifetime of hope and effort, unmet opportunities, and people he loved. He continued south along the wall, toward what he sensed was a warmer climate, all the while hoping a way down might present itself. Nothing appeared. Just the occasional explosion from below, the occasional gunfight.

And screams. Always the screams.

The land on the side of the real world rose higher against the wall, like a long, sloping bank of jumbled material, until the people and places he'd glimpsed from well over two hundred feet now stood within shouting distance, but they seemed too engrossed in their Punch and Judy dramas to notice him. He turned to check on wonderland. The gray nothingness on its outskirts seemed to have followed him, so that only a smattering of trees remained.

"No," he whispered, his heart sinking at the sight of his dissipating dream. The wall north of where he stood had also vanished into a vague impression. He rushed back in that direction, but the wall didn't reform or solidify in tandem with his steps, and so he stopped short, lest he evaporate himself. He had no choice but to travel south, and so he did.

Elroy's shoulders slumped as the land to his right rose higher against the wall. He'd reached a residential area—an endless row of back yards, in fact—and had he chosen, he could have jumped down into any one of them, then wandered off in search of his former life. To his relief, no violence had followed him into this working-class neighborhood, where summer seemed to have arrived, given the sweltering heat. He caught the scent of warm grass, along with the sound of children at play.

One back yard had a swimming pool, its water the color of algae. Another looked like a jungle, with weeds and foxtails engulfing a rusted swing set. The voices grew louder, and Elroy slowed his approach. His mother's back yard came into view, clean and trimmed, as it had been when his father was alive and well enough to care for it. Two children—a boy, aged five, and a girl who appeared several years older—kicked a deflated ball back and forth beneath the covered patio. The boy was Elroy, and the girl his sister, Monica. Impossible as it seemed, there they stood, and Elroy watched them both, his heart breaking for this little moment lost to time. Monica had died in a car accident ten short years later, and it was the first time he'd seen her since, apart from the pictures he kept. And where was home? Ah, yes, the apartment—an eight hundred square-foot box that got too hot in summer and too cold in winter, and where bedtime was dread time, because he slept alone, fearing all the while his living conditions represented the sum of his achievements. Thankfully, it hadn't been. He'd found Elysium, even if only for a sweet interlude.

Elroy watched his younger incarnation run toward the ball, wind up, then trip over his shoelaces. The boy Elroy fell face-first, palms slapping hard on the concrete. Monica rushed to his aid, then helped him up.

"You're okay," she reassured him, stopping the tears before they came. "Barely a scrape. See?"

"Can you tie my shoes?" young Elroy said, still shaken. He then blew into his palms to cool the burns.

"I already showed you how."

"I forgot," he admitted.

"No, you didn't. Watch. You take the first shoelace in this hand, then the other one like this..."

Elroy, the elder on the wall, watched himself remember how to tie his shoelaces with Monica's help, and her simple act of love and kindness left him in tears. Had she first not taught him how tie laces, he might not have learned anything at all. He absorbed every detail of this long-forgotten moment, and committed it to memory, because he couldn't stay. The moment had been lived, the real world created, and all its mysteries laid over with concrete.

Elroy took a breath, closed his eyes and envisioned his true home (his companion, the trees, the pond, and realms yet discovered), then allowed himself to fall backward.

What should have been a high, bone-crushing leap ended in less than a second, with Elroy landing hard on his back, but not so hard as to damage anything vital.

He looked up. Twilight loomed above him, alluring as ever, the constellations blinking their excitement at his return. The wall from which he'd fallen loomed well over two hundred feet above him once again. Elroy chuckled, then cheered, and wiped away his tears. "Thank you, thank you, thank you!"

He stood without issue, his legs strong and flexible, then reached up and touched his horns. Still there!

His companion called out to him, her voice strained with

worry, but before he turned to find her, he spotted a fissure in the wall they'd failed to cover. It was so small as to be imperceptible. Looking through required great effort, but no matter how hard he tried, the image wouldn't hold. He stepped away, focused his eyes on the tip of a black branch, then the stars beyond it. The trick seemed to worked, as the image through the wall became solid and steady. He once again saw himself and Monica playing in the back yard. He vowed to keep this area a secret, and visit it whenever he felt the need to remind himself that everything beyond the wall wasn't so terrible.

As for going back, he put that notion far from his mind, and thought instead about what new discoveries the day might hold.

LATENT SENSATION

The body remembers what the mind forgets
Her hair, interlaced between his fingers
Softer than aphrodisiac magic and summer gossamer
Now sleeping alone, his fingers curl inward
Grasping night, grasping nothingness
Like the legs of a dying spider
Fallen from its web

CUPID'S ARROW

Cupid's arrow is barbed
And cannot be removed without terrible consequences
Best to leave it in
Let the wound heal around it
Then snap the shaft when you're good and ready
Maybe when the next arrow flies
You'll be quick enough to catch it
But this requires great skill
And very few master the technique
So good luck
And may all your wounds
Heal over time

ALL WE WANT

All we want is…

One great song
One great poem
One great painting
One Great Love
The rest is furniture
And appliances

All we really want is…

One Great Love

If not that, then nothing above

RAZOR

AUDREY NEVER THOUGHT of Thomas as interesting or clever, but there he stood, hunched and shirtless in the corner of her darkened bedroom, his deep-set eyes collecting shadow, until he acquired a Reaper's appearance.

A living skull, she mused, full of death's secrets.

She leaned back against the headboard, folded her nude, tattooed frame into an exotic piece of origami, and lit a cigarette, observing this odd phenomenon through squinted eyes. Death pulled a pair of business casual slacks up each knotted knee, each cadaverous thigh, then cinched the waistband around his soft middle and buttoned up.

Any second he'd make a somber pronouncement about the number of the day's dead he collected and ferried off to the hereafter, but then he stepped into a bar of jaundiced light seeping through the blinds, and the death's head illusion fell apart.

A balding, middle-aged man of minor authority—a *John,* and nothing more—offered her a satisfied grin, and said, "That was pretty good, wasn't it?"

She didn't return the smile, nor answer the question.

Instead, she wondered why he kept what little hair remained on the sides of his head, and why his wife didn't demand that he do something about the tiny tufts of hair crouching in his ears, like tarantulas Maybe she'd do the poor woman a favor and tell him it looked disgusting, and to trim it.

"You're hot just sitting there, you know that?" he said, buttoning his shirt with post-coital sobriety.

"Am I?"

"Oh, come on, it's impossible for you not to be hot. Trust me, all the guys that go for the glamour girls with fake boobs and huge asses have no idea what they're missing."

"Lucky you," she said.

"But you're still young and don't appreciate it, and that's hot, too."

"I'm twenty-nine. That's thirty-nine in man years."

"It's young," he asserted. "The smoking, though. No one smokes anymore."

"Just dirty little whores," she replied, all innocence.

"What? Oh, *that*. I didn't mean that. Not in the way you think. I just got swept up in the moment. It's your fault, you know. You make me crazy," he said, grinning. "You should take it as a compliment."

She dismissed the idea of telling him about the hair in his ears. Let him walk around like a fool. Let the people recoil in horror, then whisper and point.

He padded down his pockets, found what jingled there, and said, "Come on, you know I'd never want to hurt you. I didn't mean it that way, babe."

"Babe? That's new."

"You're being ridiculous. Come here. Audrey, please," he said, opening his arms in welcome.

She'd earned her cigarette break, and had no intentions of entertaining any further demands, but Thomas (the Tuesday Man, she called him) had proven himself a reliable client. He paid well, tipped well, and often came bearing gifts; and apart from mothball kisses, and a fetish of dropping to his knees and huffing her backside, he had predictable, pedestrian habits. Not only that, he almost always finished fast. Yes, best to keep him on call.

She snuffed her cigarette and went to him, then dropped her arms to her sides, awaiting his embrace.

"Closer," he said, his voice huskier.

She approached, then submitted to his affections. He trapped her in his arms, smelled her hair, which covered half of her face like a purple, feathery fan, and kissed the top of her head.

"You're gorgeous. I could watch you for hours," he said, caressing a carnival-esque tattoo on the underside of her wrist. "If I could afford it, you wouldn't have to work for anyone else. You'd be all mine. Would you like that?"

"I don't think you know what you're asking," she said.

"Yes, I do. If I could, I'd just pack it all up and take you with me."

Another *if*, not that it mattered. "You're a bad boy, Thomas, but not that bad. You're too loyal."

"Are you so sure?"

"That, and I think you're afraid."

"Oh, really, young lady. Afraid of what?" he asked, chuckling.

"I don't know… losing everything?"

That ended the laughter. "Okay, you've had your revenge. Well done. I need to get going," he said, releasing her. "I'm out of town next week, so maybe we'll pick it up later."

"You know where to find me."

Thomas strode down the hall, whistling, and she locked the dead bolt behind him. Not long after, hollowness crept in, though she didn't long for anyone's company. She had a habit of falling prey to the vampirism of the needy, and it always left her drained, no matter the precautions she took, or the mantras she repeated.

She returned to the suffocating confines of her bedroom—still ripe with Thomas's musk—and opened a window. Outside, Downtown Los Angeles hummed a continuous, toxic note, and blew its smog-tinged breath through the blinds. She lit a trio of candles on the dresser, and her thoughts turned toward the jewelry box there, and the prospect of oblivion contained within. No, not the prospect: the promise.

She opened the lid with a priest's reverence for holy objects, and slid her fingertip over agate, opal, and cubic zirconia settings, but almost every ring in her collection lacked the charge of true nostalgia. She caressed more bits of brilliance, until her finger came upon the rounded back edge of a razor blade, snug and secure between black velvet pads, and slouched among all those pretty things like a murderer attending Sunday Mass.

She removed it, and the friction of release produced a faint whisper: "*Free*," the razor seemed to say. She held it between thumb and forefinger, admiring the instrument's simplicity—one side for holding, the other for cutting. Then came a familiar vision: her face, half-submerged in steaming bathwater, a crimson cloud spreading outward beneath it, as she slipped down, down… mouth, nose, then the eyes, closed and looking inward, her purple hair swirling about like alien kelp; then, stillness, with only the slow drip, drip, drip of the faucet to mark the passage of time.

How long would it take them to find her body? A week? Two?

"I'll be a rotting Venus," she whispered, "but not yet." She refused to leave Thomas with the impression that he'd somehow hastened her departure, and wouldn't he mourn with pride for having achieved the ultimate conquest? "She chose suicide over living without me. Damn waste of a good lay, if you ask me," he'd tell his golf buddies.

No, Audrey imagined her exit as a tiptoed affair, like someone slipping out of a party unnoticed, the guests all sensing a change in atmosphere, but failing to put a face or name to it. Leave a mystery. Leave a black hole that swallows in questions and tears and theories, she thought, before sliding the razor back into place and closing the lid.

She showered Thomas off her skin, dressed to impress no one, then entered the sanctuary of her living room and threw the curtains wide. Los Angeles at night had once dazzled her, but the twinkling lights had lost their charm. She knew what slithered through the city's streets, freeway underpasses, and alleys. She'd skipped over ponds of urine, and had seen a man stabbed over a dispute about a hamburger. She'd walked in a meth-induced haze among the mad, who screamed at the sky, or spat at invisible enemies, and had come to understand their secret language. She'd been held down behind a dumpster by two grimy vagrants ripe with disease, their exposed genitals peeling with filth, and had escaped by sheer providence.

And just in case she'd forgotten how romantic the city could be, her neighbors struck up an argument that swelled to full-scale battle in minutes. They tumbled room-to-room, slamming doors and banging on doors between shouts. Then came the tears and apologies. Midsummer romance. It made her sick.

She reached for the television remote with the intention of drowning them out, when her phone rang.

"Shit," she said, cursing the phone, and then her absent-mindedness. She'd forgotten about her nine o'clock appointment. She almost never booked two in the same evening, as much for practical reasons as for physical, but at the time she'd made the decision she needed the extra money. To complicate matters, she'd never met the man Joy had recommended to her, and he might make any number of unexpected requests. She indulged most, but she had limits, and those limits had increased with each passing year.

The phone's display darkened, and the call disappeared to the cemetery of voicemail. Let him find someone else to play with tonight, she concluded, wiping her hands of the matter.

She lit a cigarette and pointed the remote at the TV, and just before she pressed the on-button, three gentle knocks, followed by fourth a few seconds later, came to her door. The code. The combination. Her appointment had arrived. She froze, and hoped he'd grow tired of waiting and wander home. No such luck. The knocked combination came again, louder. "Shit, shit, shit," she said, in less than a whisper. She walked on cat's feet toward the door, then leaned in and listened, her ears straining through solid oak.

"I know you're in there," came a young, melodious voice on the other side. "I can feel you there. You're hardly breathing, but there's no reason to hide. It's a little childish."

She thought of Teddy, her stump-necked neighbor who'd offered to protect her in exchange for "a little taste," and who'd be more than happy to break this guy's arm if she asked, but she didn't want that kind of attention, either from her neighbors, or from Teddy.

"And now you're thinking of how to get rid of me," he said. "I haven't made the best first impression, have I? First impressions are everything, but then you don't know me, and you don't know how much money I have." Then his voice squeezed its way through the doorjamb. "But I know you, Tracey. Tracey Carlson."

She'd left that name behind nine years ago; left it to hang like a rumor over estranged family members and friends who knew her then as plain Tracey from Plano, Texas. "Go away," she warned, deepening her voice.

"There she is."

"I don't care who you are. I don't care what you think you know or want. Go away or you'll be lucky to crawl away. Your choice."

"But I come on good recommendation. Joy, your friend at the club, she told you I was a little weird but harmless, right? I am harmless, and promise to be a perfect gentleman. And I'm sure the weird thing is nothing new to you."

True, in both cases, but too much marijuana had stunted Joy's judgment, and Audrey had no idea if she'd vetted him. "Just go away, please."

"Here, Audrey. You prefer Audrey, right? A little something to let you know I'm serious."

A soft, slithering sound drew her eyes toward a pale sliver of light beneath the door. One-by-one, crisp one-hundred-dollar bills slipped through and gathered at her toes—one hundred, two hundred, three hundred. She kneeled down and picked one up, holding it toward the lamp. The security strip inside shone through the dyed parchment. The bills kept coming... seven hundred, eight hundred, nine hundred. One more slid halfway through, did a little dance, then joined the others.

"You get the other half when you let me in," he whispered.

The other half? One thousand dollars represented a good night's work, two thousand a windfall, but accepting it could introduce greater problems.

"Okay, Moneybags, here's the deal: Come back tomorrow night, same time, and you won't regret it. That's my offer." The questions poured in while she awaited his answer. Who was he? How did he know her real name? Was he psychotic? And if he had such deep pockets, then why hadn't Joy kept him to herself?

"You're not playing fair."

"Or don't come back at all, and chalk it up to one hell of an expensive lesson."

He shuffled behind the door, then sighed. "Fine. Tomorrow."

"Yes, tomorrow."

"You'll make it special, something I won't forget? And you'll be here, won't you?"

"Very special, and yes."

"I'll trust you to keep your word. Good evening, Miss Carlson. Tracey. Audrey."

His brisk steps receded down the hallway, then disappeared. She lunged for her cell phone and texted Joy.

The new guy. WTF?!?!

Joy didn't reply. In fact, she didn't reply to any text messages or calls that night, deepening Audrey's concern to the point of genuine alarm.

Audrey swam through a roiling black ocean and toward a distant shoreline, but the harder she paddled, the farther it receded from sight. The current carried her sideways, until she found herself on the outside edge of a deep vortex, the black, misty center of which produced a cylindrical howl. It swept her along faster, each revolution taking her down, down, until the blackness beneath her gaped wide. She broke free of the water's influence, and found herself in free fall. Then down she went into darkness, screaming and groping for purchase.

She awoke kicking the blankets from her legs in a cold sweat, and by degrees she gained a sense of equilibrium. No ocean, no void; just her room, pale blue with early morning light. Loneliness had never been much of a problem, but it seemed so then. Something else occurred to her: she'd fought against the current and encroaching darkness, and didn't that suggest she still possessed the instinct to live?

The previous night's experience with her odd visitor pushed the question from her mind. She then recalled fragments of what Joy had said about him before going off grid. "He's a pretty boy... a little weird, but harmless... might be loaded."

A little weird, but harmless. How did he know what Joy had told her? She checked her phone. No response. Stranger still, no one else had heard from Joy.

She downed her coffee in three blistering gulps, showered, and dressed, then set out into traffic with the hope of finding answers.

The Royal Palms apartment complex—a lime green box set between sagging 1930's bungalows—lacked the two key elements to justify its lofty name: palm trees and anything resembling royalty. It did have a secured entrance, however. She input Joy's code into the intercom and waited. Nothing. After the third failed attempt, a white-haired woman in bright hues appeared in the courtyard, and willed a small terrier testing the length of its leash toward the gate.

"Pepper, come. Pepper," she said, opening the door.

Audrey made herself small and non-threatening. "He's a cutie."

The woman appraised Audrey with fierce old eyes. The verdict: undesirable. Pepper made for a patch of ivy. "Pepper, come. Get your little butt over here!" she commanded, tugging on his leash.

Audrey caught the door before it closed, stepped in, and flitted past a series of curtained windows and doors toward number seventeen. She doubted she'd find Joy at home, but had nothing to lose by getting a closer look. As expected, Joy didn't answer when she knocked. Groping for ideas, she tried the doorknob, and to her surprise, it turned. She stepped into stale coolness and blue shadow, shut the door behind her, then stood there a moment widening her pupils. Joy had left signs of herself everywhere—the clothes on the floor, the cluttered kitchen table, the bottles on the sink, and the dirty litter box by the wall heater, potent, even from a distance.

"Hey, you here?"

The refrigerator answered with a grating hum, then a shape slunk out of the darkness in the hall and took the form of a cat. "Charley, where's your mama, huh?" Charley approached and wound between her ankles in silken figure eights, sharing the secrets of solitude with gentle purrs. "Where is she?"

Charley followed her into the bedroom. The bed resembled an empty cocoon. Clothing and shoes piled on the floor. The adjoining bathroom held no traces of moisture, or the lingering scent of spritzed perfume. Overall, nothing caused immediate alarm, and she thought to leave, but then her eyes fell upon Joy's computer desk. Among the papers and unwashed mugs lay Joy's collection of sex toys—some ponderous, others slim, sleek, and translucent. Above the desk: a webcam, its lens pointed toward the empty chair, where Audrey knew Joy entertained her on-line followers. "Three thousand strong and growing," she'd once bragged, before urging Audrey to do the same, which would free her from physical contact with customers.

Audrey sat down and wiggled the mouse. The computer's monitor brightened. Joy had been looking at health and beauty articles, images of deep green forests, and a personality quiz. One by one she closed the pages, but paused when the final window revealed Audrey's own live, high-definition image staring off-camera. She traced the source of that image to the webcam, and turned it toward the wall. She then looked through a list of saved videos, and came across what she expected—Joy, pulling her audience in and keeping them there as long as possible, then making digital rain with a rousing, writhing finale.

She'd seen enough, but her instincts led her to open the final video. A still frame Joy sent a chill through her body. She looked like an escaped cult member, the trauma of her experience reflected in her eyes, her unkempt her. Audrey pressed the play button and the video started, but no sound accompanied the image. She paused it, adjusted the volume, and played it again.

"How many times do you want me to say it?" Joy asked an unknown person on the other end of the camera. Audrey didn't discern a reply, but Joy closed her eyes, as if she'd just received terrible news. She made some kind of internal adjustment, took a faltering breath, then opened her eyes once again. "I love you," she said, sincerity and hope melting to sorrow. "Why don't you believe me?" Her tears turned to sobs that shook her shoulders.

Audrey had seen every shade of Joy's moods, but vulnerability of this magnitude came as a revelation, and seeing it open and raw felt more intrusive that anything Joy could have revealed with her body and her toys. Her tears subsided in waves, and in the calm that followed, Joy looked into the lens with lifeless eyes, and said, "I take it all back. I don't love you. I fucking hate you."

The video ended.

It left Audrey shaking. She replayed it again and again, looking and listening for any clues, no matter how minute, that might illuminate the source of Joy's pain. Nothing presented itself, but Audrey knew this: Joy had been in turmoil before she disappeared. She refilled Charley's food and water bowls, enough for a few days at her best guess, then carried that haunting image of Joy with her into the bright afternoon.

. . .

She pulled into the parking lot of Delirium, a windowless, black and pink gentleman's club where she danced every Friday, and parked next to Paul's new Mercedes, which had become a source of bitterness among the staff, Audrey included. He'd inherited the club from his dad, Big Mike, and had since let it go to pot, but the decline in business hadn't stopped him from spending money like some kind of back-alley baron.

She found him sitting behind his desk in the back office, and pointing his phone toward something in the room. She tapped on the door and stepped inside, and the subject of Paul's video froze with her fingertips on her bra straps, the goods underneath still hidden. The homegrown, dishwater blonde glanced between Paul and Audrey, like some ingénue seeking approval from her audience.

Oh, sweetheart, Audrey thought, you're doomed.

"Little Audrey Hepburn. What are you doing here?" Paul asked in a buzzard's voice. He looked thirty-five, but dressed like a nineteen-year-old, his ball cap worn at a sideways tilt. "Keep going, honey," he told the girl, who resumed removing her bra. "Okay," he said, somewhat satisfied by the appearance of her breasts.

"I can see why you didn't answer your phone. Have you heard from Joy?"

"No, and she flaked out on me last night. That's strike three —hell, strike ten as far as I'm concerned."

"You're not worried?"

"Uh, nope," he said, popping the *P*.

Audrey assumed the 'nope' meant that he'd just found Joy's replacement. "When was the last time you talked to her?"

"I don't know. Three days ago, maybe."

"And?"

"And what?"

"Did she say anything that made you think she might be in trouble? Did she sound like she was upset?"

"She sounded like she always sounds—a dingbat. And you know what, I'm getting pretty sick of dealing with everyone's bullshit. This is a business, not a flop house." Then, to the girl, "Come on, come on."

"Take it easy," Audrey told him.

"I am," he said, lifting his legs onto the desk and leaning back in his chair.

The girl half-danced to imaginary music and unbuttoned her shorts, but stopped short of dropping them.

Paul lowered his phone. "This is full nude, all right? Full nude. The whole body. If you think this is hard, you'll never make it up there."

"Sorry, I can do it," the girl said, resuming her awkward routine. The shorts came down, then the panties.

Paul stared in disappointment, then said, "No. Don't do it like you're about to sit on the damn toilet. Take your time. Shake it around like it's worth something. Get those jerks reaching into their pockets *before* you show them the cookie. Start over."

"So, you don't care what happened to her?"

"I'm sorry, what were we talking about?" he said.

"Screw you."

"Relax, she'll turn up."

Audrey headed down the hall, and Paul's voice echoed close behind. "I expect you to be here Friday. Don't be a flake. I hate flakes."

But Friday lurked on the edge of a distant future, and she had more pressing concerns to address.

She arrived home and replayed Joy's video in memory while straightening up a month's worth of neglect. The job of cleaning, scrubbing, and organizing helped her clarify her thoughts. She'd see Moneybags and do her best to get some answers from him, and return his down payment, if necessary. Either way, if Joy hadn't made herself known by morning, she'd file a missing persons report, then contact everyone in Joy's circle of fair-weather friends, even her on-line followers, though she had no idea how she'd go about doing it.

Job finished, she prepared her body and hardened her mind, then went to the nightstand drawer in the bedroom and removed the plastic safety guard on a can of bear spray that boasted a range of twenty-five feet. She'd burn a hole through her visitor's skull if things got out of hand. She then went around the room and lit some candles.

Not long after, three knocks reached her ears; then, after a pause, the fourth.

Audrey had known handsome men, charming men, men with playground bodies, but the one standing in her doorway surpassed them all in mystery and allure.

"Hello," she said, suppressing mild shock. She could look and look and never see the totality of him, yet she'd seen him before—*versions* of him, anyway—in old black and white movies. There stood the tragic hero mourning a lost love, the innocent suspect eluding the detective, the high-stakes gambler outwitting angry mobsters. The tailored blacks and grays he wore added to the effect. Cooper, Bogey, Dean—he looked like all of them, only real, and tall, and angular, and...

...she mustn't let it affect her judgment. "Come in," she said.

His eyes, though an enchanting blue, concealed all thought; they just observed, and she found it chilling. He leaned forward with each step, as though piloting his thin frame required a certain amount of momentum, and stepped inside. His eyes went to some of the objects and furnishings in the room, and he smiled, as though he'd confirmed a suspicion about her.

A black leather bag slung over his shoulder (large enough to carry any number of murderous instruments) set off an alarm inside her head.

"I see your game," she said.

"Game?" he asked, regarding her with those damned eyes that seemed to contain an ocean.

"Yes." She changed her voice into something like that of a voiceover announcer, and said, "He enters the room, but he does not look at her, he does not say hello. He's used to the way women look at him, and he uses his little gift to make them feel uncertain."

"I make you feel uncertain? That's not my intention."

"You said you'd be a perfect gentleman, and gentleman are supposed to be polite. Have a seat."

"By all means," he replied, following her instructions with something close to delight. He sat on the sofa and placed the bag between his legs, then awaited her next command.

She lit a cigarette. "And who in the hell says 'by all means'?" She held up an envelope containing his down payment, and he seemed to recognize it. "It's all here. You can have it back, but I want you to be honest with me."

"I don't care about the money, assuming that's what you're holding, but you can ask me anything you like. I'm an open book," he said, parting his hands.

"Tell me about Joy."

"Joy," he announced, his eyes glancing toward a disappointing memory. "Predictably pretty, predictable in every way. She wasn't a very good subject."

"Subject? What do you mean?"

"She's a young soul lost in an old world. It's in the eyes, a kind of constant surprise and confusion. Everything is new and terrifying. No, she wasn't right at all for my work. It demands a flat recognition—acceptance, if you will—of one's position, of the futility of..."

"Go on."

"...the futility of living," he said.

The statement landed hard, and the adrenaline followed. "Where is she?"

"I have no clue, nor do I have any interest. I saw her only one time, and that was several days ago. She understood why I wasn't interested in pursuing the arrangement further, and gave me your information. In that time, I did some research on you."

"And why go through all the trouble?"

"No trouble. Just research."

"Research," she stated.

"That's right. I take my work seriously. I don't pick just anyone."

His claim of professionalism did little to ease her suspicions. "And what is your work?"

By way of reply, he unzipped the bag with long fingers that were made for probing the undiscovered regions of a woman's soul. Her fascination competed with her urge to run to her room, get the bear spray, and light him up. Just before fear took complete hold of her, the stranger removed a still camera and held it up for inspection.

Audrey almost cried with relief.

"What is it?" he asked, his lips curling at the corners into something like a smile.

"I can't tell if this is some kind of act, or if you really are this weird."

"I've been accused of much worse," he said.

The camera hid most of his face. *Click*. He lowered it, then tilted his head. "Stand over there by the window and take off your clothes." He delivered the instruction as though he were a doctor seeing the last patient at the end of a long day.

She removed one of her rings.

"No," he said. "Leave the jewelry on." *Click, click, click.*

"What do you plan to do with these?" she asked, in regard to the photos.

"If I like what I see—" *click* "—I'll add you to my collection."

"This town is full of professional models. Why not just hire one of them?" She removed her top, then unlatched her bra.

"It's not..." His eyes drifted toward her breasts, though the look lacked the lecherous zeal she'd seen so often before. He studied them with something like philosophical wonder. *Click.* "It's not the same. Put your arms down and look right into the lens, as if you'd just told me to get out, and no longer want to see me. Yeah, that's it."

A thin layer of sweat appeared on his forehead. The heat could have caused it, but it didn't explain how his energy contracted inward, how his fingertips whitened as they gripped the camera, or how his eyes darkened a shade. "Did you know that your shoulders slant to the left ever so slightly?"

"Yes," she said, wondering if he used photography as a role-playing ploy. In fact, she doubted he'd been taking pictures at all, though she didn't want to spoil the fun by asking.

He stepped in closer, and lengthened the lens. "Hold very still."

Click.

His soothing voice went to work on her senses, and she admired his clear instructions. The clicking continued until she removed her pants and set them aside.

Silence.

He lowered the camera, studying her—toes, ankles, knees, and thighs, and then his eyes slid toward the inward curve of her sex, still veiled by her panties. They lingered there, a war between desire and clinical objectivity raging behind them.

He's frightened, her instincts told her.

He adjusted the lens and moved in for tighter shots.

She offered a clear invitation to intimacy with her eyes, then pulled at the waistband of her panties with her thumbs.

"Not yet," he said, raising a hand to stop her. He dabbed his forehead with a sleeve. "Turn around and pull them down from behind."

Audrey turned. She knew the rhythm of this dance, and when to take lead. She bent over, maintaining an inward arch in her lower back, then took her panties down, inch by inch. She shifted her weight from one leg to the other, aware that this subtle motion provided him a peek of the most secretive part of her body. She sensed him drawing closer, and then he fired away.

"You have a dancer's body," he said. "It's remarkable." He made some kind of mechanical adjustment to the camera.

"Isn't it too dark in here?" she asked, looking at the starless sky through a narrow part in the curtains.

"No. Stand up and turn around. Slowly."

She stood upright maintaining the arch in her back, then turned with the expectation that he'd at least unbuttoned his shirt, but he looked more nervous than he had moments before.

"Sit on the sofa and spread your legs," he said.

She sat, putting a palm on each knee. With a devil-knows-best gaze, she parted her legs and leaned back. He choked back a breath and raised the camera once more.

He moved in closer, closer, his finger working the shutter with manic dexterity. He adjusted the lens, then confirmed with both eyes that the woman he'd been photographing existed as something more than just a mirage captured on celluloid. He dropped to his knees and fell into the universe of her parted legs, his expression a cubist's rendering of conflicting emotions.

She willed the camera toward her body, and toward the deepest part of her being. Let him see. Don't hide anything. She gave him pain and desire in equal amounts. She gave him the blackest of days and the brightest of childhood hopes, long buried, but recalled afresh. She told him about the dangerous secret she kept hidden in the jewelry box, but only with her eyes.

Click.

Can you save me? she asked, with a tilt of her head.

Click.

Can you help me forget who I am?

Click.

Do you have the strength to show me your fears?

Click.

I'll soothe them. I promise.

And still he clicked away. The heat from his hands radiated toward her thighs. Each captured frame of light felt to her like a kiss on the lower abdomen. She caught his scent: anise and stardust, sage and sun-cracked earth. Wetness came. She salivated for his tongue, hoping to suck every lie he'd ever told from it.

He lowered the camera; then, with some apprehension, reached toward her thigh. Audrey expected icy fingers, but they'd been dipped in fire. He withdrew his hand with a start, as though he'd just placed it over an open flame, then stood and backed away, leaving a cool space between them. It swirled there, like a false winter.

"Thank you," he said, snapping on the lens cover.

The abruptness of his retreat left her bemused, perplexed, and disappointed, but not discouraged, nor cold. She rose and drew close to him, then looked through his eyes toward the person inside—the hidden person. She saw a young boy standing at the edge of a swimming pool, fearful of jumping in. She projected understanding, reassurance, desire.

"You must think I'm ridiculous," he said.

"Not at all."

"Oh, but I am. I have strict rules about mixing business with pleasure."

"That's a shame," she said, taking the camera from him and setting it down. "There's nothing wrong with holding someone, is there?" She put her arms around him, and he didn't protest or pull away; rather, he resisted by standing still, his body tense.

Then, as if by some cosmic trick, the power went out in the apartment. Block-by-block the city darkened, hurtling them into vast, empty space, and he put his arms around her in the ensuing silence, as though the cover of darkness had given him permission to break his own rules. His body relaxed into hers, contour to contour. Audrey no longer feared this man, and sensed that he didn't judge or pity her, and that his interest in her ran deeper than a pornographer's skin-deep fixation. The previous withdrawal of his hand had disturbed her, but his embrace deepened, suggesting something inside him had broken free: that little boy, maybe, jumping into the water at last.

He held her in wordless wonder for several minutes, his breath easy. Her heartbeat matched its rhythm, the darkness around them setting the mood for this strange, unexpected union. She'd long understood that people spoke with their bodies, and his words came through, in the sweeping of his hand across her lower back, and into the warm curve of her buttocks. *I want to know you. I want to know what's inside you.* The words: clear as day.

And though she'd shared her body with more men than she cared to recall, she'd never shared her trust. She offered it now, or maybe he'd lifted it out of her. The sensation terrified her, this weightlessness, and every instinct shouted in her ears to run. But she didn't pull away.

Then the microwave oven beeped, the refrigerator sputtered to life, and lamplight obliterated the magic of darkness. But he held onto her—tighter than before, in fact—and it lent solidity to the ephemeral moment they'd shared, along with proof that she hadn't imagined the subtle shift toward freedom within him.

Though it never went further than a hug, his embrace comforted her throughout the night, and lingered well into morning. She flipped two fried eggs, and said, "Ryan," just to hear how his name sounded in the kitchen. And didn't saying it make him real? Yes, she concluded—too real. He hadn't volunteered his last name, or much about his personal life, and so her imagination had gone to work, filling in all those blank spaces with life experiences, traits, beliefs, old loves, his deepest hurts, and new hopes. The most prominent image: the two of them talking and getting to know each other better.

He kept his word and paid her the additional one thousand dollars, which meant a couple of weeks of solitude, if she chose, but she didn't want solitude. She wanted to see him again, if for no other reason than to peel back the enigma, though she feared the photo shoot had been a one-off session, and that he'd soon disappear back into his life, and forget about her.

A message from Joy popped up on her phone: *Hey u. I'm ok. Chillin in Santa Barbara.*

Audrey responded with: *Bitch! U had me worried!!!*

Sorry. Talk later, Joy texted back.

What about Charley?

Joy didn't reply, and Audrey assumed that Joy had made arrangements for someone to look after him, which might also explain why she'd left her front door unlocked. She'd bolted out of town without warning before, and so Audrey, after cursing her friend's selfishness, put the matter to rest.

After breakfast, she cyber-stalked Ryan using every word combination she could conjure, but each search led her down a path of useless information. Did he live in his mother's basement? Not likely. Was he a jet-setting playboy who took perverse pleasure in slumming around the lower classes? Maybe. Was he a tortured artist, abstinent and lonely and haunted by failure? She must find out.

Accepting temporary defeat, she went out to do some grocery shopping, but it seemed the world had changed overnight. She marveled at all the cars, and the streetlights cycling through their colors, conducting the flow of traffic. The machine that spat out a parking slip at the public garage struck her as a strange, mechanical beast sticking out its tongue. The rows of shopping carts pushed into each other in front of the market appeared as nesting dolls, or maybe people, all jammed into each other's lives, head to tail, head to tail.

She wandered through the supermarket's gleaming aisles in amazement. Someone had organized all the products by predictive consumer habits. How clever of them! Most of all she noticed the people, their closed faces concealing Kabuki theatres of mind, as they squeezed the tomatoes and smelled the limes. Eye contact with others: a sin, punishable by death. She'd sleepwalked among them for years, but the order had been disrupted. Yes, a beautiful creature had shuttled her off into the dark, lifted her out of herself, and revealed to her the graveyard dance of blind routine.

In short: nothing looked the same.

She returned home and found an envelope taped to her door. The name *Audrey* had been written on it in elegant cursive; below that, the letter *R*, suggesting two things: that Ryan had put it there, and that he preferred her invented identity to the name of Tracey. Or maybe he understood that *she* preferred it. Either way, she appreciated the gesture. She smiled for the first time in weeks, took it inside, then settled on the sofa and read.

The light of true beauty cannot remain hidden. It must be elevated like a beacon for wayward vessels.

—R.

Her first impression: he'd written it to the wrong person. It had to be a mistake, or maybe just a cruel joke, though it seemed sincere, and didn't that make it worse?

The light of true beauty? What light? What beauty?

She was the midnight creeper who kept company with scarecrow men. She was the penetrated, the used, the plastic doll smeared in petroleum jelly, and she never had any illusions about being anything else. She did it for freedom, and freedom justified the cost, but a kind note consisting of two little lines put her face-to-face with a horrible truth—that she'd destroyed her life.

She read the quote again, and the loveliness of those lines dredged up every hideous aspect of her profession, and then the vast, shadowy shape of her shame rose to full height and enveloped her. She saw herself through Ryan's eyes, and imagined what it must have taken him to see beyond all her ugliness in order to write his note. He couldn't have written it without considering the things she'd done, the way she lived, and the number of men she'd entertained. He knew, of course. He knew everything.

Stripped bare by this knowledge, Audrey succumbed to despair and cried herself empty.

She sat there for an hour, soulless and hollow, and then her old friend the razor called out to her from within the jewelry box—a faint plea she couldn't resist. Its seductive voice drew her into the bedroom. She approached the jewelry box and removed the blade. It seemed to smile, and say, *"What took you so long?"*

She always knew she would, one day. That day had come. And why not right there? Drench the carpet. Make it sticky with your life force. Let the flies come. Let the scent of your blood gag anyone who enters.

She raised the blade to her wrist and pressed a sharp corner into a vein just below the heel of her palm. It hurt more than she expected, and she bit back a cry, and then the first drop came, brilliant against her skin, like an albino rat's red eye. She held the blade in position, gathered more courage, and marked the path she intended to take with her eyes. She would not employ the coward's perpendicular strum across the strings. No, she'd drag it from wrist to elbow in three clean swipes, so that they'd never be able to stitch her back together again.

She needed out, she thought, pressing deeper. Out, out, out! The tears came, blurring her vision. "Out!" she said, her voice sounding hollow in the room. She opened her vein to a trickle, and then imagined herself stripped of skin—glorious and gleaming, a terror to behold, but bold and truthful in her new condition, and filled with rage and vengeance and fire, and beholden to no one.

No one.

No one owned her.

That is: no one owned her without her permission.

And she'd given them all permission, hadn't she? Yes, she had, going all the way back to the apocalyptic playground of her youth, where adult things happened to her during those long, unsupervised afternoons. A series of ill-considered yesses over the years had brought her to this place, to the edge of annihilation.

But what if she said no, just this once? No, I don't want your interest in me, or your need of me, or your money. Keep all of it. Choke on it. She released the pressure from her wrist, and the razor offered her a bloodstained grin. *More,* it said.

"No," she whispered.

Pat-pat-pat, came the sound of her blood dripping onto the carpet.

She realized the person she'd meant to kill sought something greater than death; she sought release from the trap she'd built for herself. A feeling of defiance welled up within her—unexpected, powerful, and resolute. In that moment the sharp object in her hand represented the men, scores of them, who fell out of the darkness of her memories and mounted her. They came faceless and marauding, bow-backed and groaning, their sweat dripping onto her body. They pinned her wrists behind her head, then lapped at the nape of her neck with foul tongues, their bodies stiffening on the edge of release, then wilting as they rolled over, making room for the next, and the next, and the next. She squeezed the razor between her fingers, focused her entire will toward it, then unleashed her pain, humiliation, and resentment into it in a single, white-hot stream. She no longer wanted the torment, nor the memories of the men, so in they went: The nervous ones with cold hands, the cheap bastards, the passionless muscle boys; in went the blue-hearted, blue-collar men, the married apologists, the rape-fetishists.

All of them, in fact, but one.

She applied pressure to her wound with some tissue, and the bleeding subsided in less than ten minutes, but one immediate problem remained: What to do about the razor? She'd never considered herself superstitious, but she'd denied the executioner its due by giving it her pain instead of her life—a dirty trick it wouldn't soon forget. And it had been so patient with her, so understanding. Now, it almost hummed with trapped energy, and she believed she'd have to perform some kind of ritual to contain that power, then find a proper place in which to bury it. The bottom of the ocean seemed suitable.

Then it occurred to her that she'd just made an extraordinary decision: She'd chosen to live. She wrapped the razor in tissue, then tucked it away inside her purse, with the intention of disposing it at the first opportunity.

Choosing life came with unexpected insights and responsibilities. She poured herself a glass of wine and jotted down all the subtle (and not so subtle) ways in which she'd punished herself over the years. The exercise offered no cathartic high, nor did it pull her down into the abyss. It left her somewhere in the purgatory of contemplation. How she'd lived so long under the harsh conditions of her own self-hatred struck her as a minor miracle. She didn't consider herself healed after finishing the list. If anything, she respected the darkness more, the same way a great fighter respects a well-matched opponent.

The darkness might come for her again, she reasoned, and she'd have to take precautions.

For six consecutive days, she arrived home to find a new note from Ryan attached to her door, and the profundity of what he wrote set her adrift into daydreams, though not the knight in shining armor variety. The notes helped her shape a new vision of herself—a future self that placed her needs first, spoke with clear intentions, and avoided at all costs the pitfalls of vice and carelessness, while presenting a more formidable figure to the world.

How he came and went without her noticing seemed like a magic trick. She considered texting him, or replying with a hand-written note, but sensed any disruption of the game might kill the fun. Besides, what would she write? *Dear Ryan, I think we're both screwed up and should be together.* No way.

Phase two of Audrey's revival consisted of cutting all ties to her underground existence. Thomas protested and pleaded for one more go at it, but when his persistence turned mean-spirited, she reminded him that she could bring his life crashing down around him with a single call to his wife. It worked better than she'd hoped, though she wouldn't have done it had he pressed her further. The man had children, after all, and why should they suffer for his sins?

So, Thomas the Tuesday Man disappeared, and then Paul and his stinking strip club sank off the coast of her concerns. The great wide future spread out before her, terrifying and unexplored, like the ocean she'd seen in her dream.

She found the final note from Ryan on her door on a sweltering Thursday evening. This one contained an invitation to dinner. A smile broke over her face, because the note read clearer than anything he'd written before it. No poetry, just pure intent. She'd never been to the restaurant he'd chosen, but a quick on-line search told her she'd better buy a new dress.

"It looks amazing on you," a young clerk wearing too much makeup said. The chance to sell Audrey one of the boutique's more expensive items had her lingering too close and asking too many questions.

Audrey had selected a powder blue dress with short sleeves and a crisp white collar: something a young woman might have worn in the mid-1940's. She stood before a triptych of mirrors, looking over her shoulder to see how it appeared from behind.

"See how it cuts up just behind the knee? Yeah, you look awesome. And the color makes your tattoos really pop," the clerk said, in clear admiration of her own fashion sense.

Audrey wondered how that might play in an upscale restaurant, then decided it didn't matter. Let people adjust to her presence, not the other way around. She turned once more, adjusting the collar and flattening out the fabric on the front, then straightened her shoulders. It felt right, and in all the right places—a rarity for any first outfit pulled from the rack.

"I'll go with it," she said.

"Awesome choice. It's a head-turner."

Audrey then selected a small clutch to complement the dress, and the evening's first fantasy about what might transpire danced through her mind. In it, Ryan laughed, then reached across the table and touched her hand. She'd said something charming. Imagine that!

She brought everything to the register and removed her wallet from her purse, and the razor—still wrapped in tissue—fell onto the glass counter. Audrey froze. The clerk's expression suggested nothing out of the ordinary had happened, but Audrey knew what the tissue contained. The men and all her suffering were in that thing, howling together.

"Miss?"

"Yes?" Audrey responded, picking up the razor, then shaking the memory of grunts and groans from her mind.

"How would you like to pay?"

"Oh, I'm sorry. Cash."

She spent another hour shopping for a pair of heels that wouldn't pinch her toes too much or cause blisters, should the night go longer than anticipated, though she had no idea what to expect. All of Ryan's notes indicated that he'd devoted a significant amount of energy in crafting them, and delivering them unseen had been a feat in its own right, but given his eccentric behavior, room for misinterpretation remained.

She came upon a small souvenir shop full of kitschy, Hollywood-themed merchandise, where a life-size image of James

Dean looked down at her from behind the glass, his eyes filled with a curious combination of strength and fragility—the same look she'd seen in Ryan's eyes when she'd parted her legs for him. It set a colony of bats loose in her stomach, and that fluttering sensation, which resonated deeper than mere excitement, triggered an internal warning: Do not think of that word, do not say that word; put that word as far from your mind as possible. Call it a crush, call it infatuation. Call it an emotional glitch brought on by loneliness, but do not entertain the possibility that it might blossom into something real. But didn't the denial of this unexpected emotion make it sweeter and more tempting? James Dean had no say on the subject. He just stood there, cool, melancholy, and unreachable.

Audrey felt like an idiot standing alone outside the restaurant, where a contingent of silver-haired power brokers and their statuesque blonde companions waited for the host to call their names, their eyes darting toward her, cataloguing, judging. She gave them a view of her back, then watched the sun collide with the horizon and bleed out red.

Ryan was fifteen minutes late. Still in the excusable zone, but not for long.

She caught a whiff of garlic and wine every time the restaurant doors opened, the diners inside talking too loud, and laughing too loud. She soon found herself alone in the dark, turning away from the headlights of oncoming cars, and pacing a little, the heels she'd bought digging in, like medieval torture boots.

Then a gentle hand touched her shoulder. "I am so sorry," came that familiar musical voice. It melted away her concerns. She turned, and there stood Ryan, looking contrite and handsome in dark jeans and a charcoal blazer, his hair piled to messy perfection. And the eyes, of course, ocean blue, and filled with regret. "I didn't mean to keep you waiting. All I wanted was for everything to go perfectly. Are you hungry?"

"A drink sounds better than food at the moment," she said.

"Well, my dear, that is a given," he said, brightening.

He took her by the arm and whisked through the doors. They weaved through the crowded waiting area and adjoining bar with little regard for anyone blocking their path, and she had to smile for the brusqueness of his technique. They plowed toward the host station, flanked on all sides by folks frothing for their first drink. The idea of getting a table seemed like a far-off fantasy. But the host, an older gentleman erudite to the point of femininity, greeted Ryan with a smile, then led both she and Ryan past the same foursome that had given Audrey a visual shake-down outside. They stood aghast at the sight of Audrey getting a table before them, and she hoped they'd stew in their own resentment for hours.

The host led them toward a small table in a somewhat secluded area, then opened his palm toward two vacant chairs. "Enjoy your evening," he said.

"You must have connections," Audrey said, sitting.

He winked, then froze as if caught by surprise. "Did I just wink at you?"

"You did," she said, laughing.

"Oh, no. I'm becoming a caricature." He eased back in his seat and ran his fingers through his hair.

"I don't see how that's possible."

"Oh, it is. Trust me. I'm sure by the end of the night I'll have run through my entire repertoire of stupid clichés and mannerisms. I'm a little nervous. Are you nervous?"

"Yes," she said, warmed by his confession.

"Thankfully, there is a cure."

The cure arrived at the table wrapped in white linen. She didn't know her way around wines, nor did she anticipate the server pouring the first glass with a kind of ritualistic fervor.

The wine came out rich and red, and struck Audrey as sacramental, and for the first time in her life she believed she understood the allure. They toasted without fanfare, and the first sip eased her into the atmosphere, the second into a mood befitting the occasion. She relaxed, and as she did, her eyes took in details she'd missed earlier. Ryan had something on his mind, something more than idle chitchat.

"I owe you an apology," he said, the candlelight glimmering in his eyes.

"Another one? Wow."

"Yes. I didn't treat you like a person when we met. I was cold. I've photographed many women in your profession, and over time I think I became jaded. No, I *know* I became jaded."

"I'm no longer in that profession."

Her statement hung there, then the fullness of it seemed to sink in. Ryan bowed his head, and said, "That's wonderful. And now I have to ask how you got into it."

She sipped her wine and let a few events from her tumultuous past bubble up from a forbidden place in her memory. At the center of it all loomed a shadow man—a man she trusted who had hurt her. "It's not a story I like to tell."

"They never are. You don't have to talk about it."

"One day I'll tell you. I promise."

"And you don't have to make any promises, either."

"No. I really want to tell you. It's just... bad, bad mojo. Really bad. The kind of bad that makes people feel the need to give you awkward apologies."

"So, you refrain from telling them as an act of courtesy."

"Not really. More like self-preservation. Anyway, you weren't cold. You were very sweet at the end."

"Were you impressed by the way I cut the power?" He said, leaning down and blowing out the candle between them.

"Very."

"You know, it's a strange thing to reveal so much to a

person without actually seeing that person. I hope my letters didn't frighten you. I think you have more guts than I do, revealing yourself so plainly."

"I don't think they're the same thing. Showing someone your body is a lot easier than showing someone your soul."

"I don't know about that," he said, betraying that same tragic look she'd seen in James Dean's eyes, "but I do know that you're beautiful, and special."

His statement rang with sincerity.

During dinner she had trouble remembering what to do with all those shiny instruments on the table. *This thing is a fork. You poke food with it. This other thing is a knife. You can use it to cut out your tongue, if you feel the sudden urge to say something dumb.*

He'd given so much of himself in letters, that the idea of showing him the terrible secret she'd transferred from her purse to the new clutch seemed a fair trade. He'd saved her, in a way, or had at least opened a door to new possibilities, but laying something that heavy on him on their first date (was it a date?) could guarantee that it would be their last, so she kept quiet about the razor and her close brush with the void.

"I want to show you how they turned out," he said.

"The photos?"

"Yes."

The word came out charged, and it sent an electric current through her body.

The first thing that happened when they stepped outside: he kissed her. The second: she fell under a spell of infatuation so deep, that it may as well have been the word she forbade herself speaking. She must not need him, she thought, savoring the taste of his lips, while burning for contact with his bare skin. No, no, no; she wouldn't allow it. Need kills, after all.

Ryan suggested that she leave her car in a public garage so they could drive together, then up they went through winding roads into the Hollywood Hills, drifting along to the sound of intertwining violins and cellos, the wine in Audrey's system getting her to hum along. His warm hand found hers, and she intertwined her fingers through his, and it felt more erotic and special than anything she'd experienced with anyone else.

She followed Ryan into the tiled foyer of his Spanish mansion, no doubt built to satisfy the moguls and stars of Hollywood's Golden Age, and her steps produced an opulent echo. Her eyes went toward the grand stairway, then followed the wrought iron banister's graceful curve toward the top floor, where chandeliers glowed with muted amber light through curved archways.

"This way," he said, setting his keys in an ornate bowl by the door.

She followed him into an open room designed for entertaining elites. Small treasures from around the world (many of them erotic) adorned the shelves, each fighting for attention with elephantine appendages and ponderous breasts, bulging eyes and elongated tongues. The expensive furniture, original artwork, and architectural detail suggested she'd just stepped into a museum, where she could look, but not touch anything. She turned, and realized Ryan had been watching her the whole time.

"It can be a little overwhelming the first time you see it, but it's just stuff," he said. "My designer picked out most of it. She's good at finding these little oddities for me, but I think I've gone overboard with it. What do you think?"

"It'll do," Audrey said, with a touch of sarcasm. She approached a shelf, and her interest gravitated toward an odd sculpture that, at first glance, seemed to her a tawdry, nightmare circus come to life, but closer inspection revealed a sinister wit at play. A circus ringleader stood atop a high platform, whip in hand, as though poised to strike; below him, five obese, nude women in descending amounts of girth had given birth to one another, like nesting dolls in reverse.

"Some people see that and leave, but not before leveling accusations of misogyny against me."

"I can see why."

"A woman made that," he said. "I explain that to them, along with the artist's intention, but it does no good. Once you engage the emotions, reason flies out the window. Anyway, I didn't bring you here to look at all these ridiculous objects. I brought you here for a very specific reason."

"Oh, yeah?"

"Oh, yes," he said, sliding back a heavy door to reveal a wet bar. "This is what people miss when they leave in a huff." He stepped behind the bar, and removed two glasses from a shelf. "I'm guessing you're a vodka girl."

"Good guess."

He took his time mixing two colorful cocktails. "I know what you must be thinking, or wondering… 'Where does he get the money?'"

She crossed an expanse of Spanish tile to meet him at the counter. "The thought crossed my mind," she said, sitting at a stool, "but it's none of my business."

"Okay, but I'll tell you this: after you make a certain amount, it begins to multiply while you sleep. To be honest, I don't know exactly where it comes from anymore."

"I don't believe that."

"It's true. It's almost absurd," he said, handing her a drink, then raising his glass for a toast.

She clinked her glass against his and took a sip. The bittersweet flavor disguised any underlying harshness, and warm currents of euphoria radiated from her chest outward. "This is... dangerous."

"Dangerous in a good way, I hope."

"It is."

"So, are you ready?" A change had come over his expression, subtle as a darkening cloud, but she caught it.

"I don't know. I don't know if I'm ready to see myself that way right now. The thought of me spreading my legs on a wall in this house is a little unsettling."

"Oh, but no one else has ever seen it. I have a studio. Actually, it's more of what I would call a creative space." He seemed to register her apprehension, then said, "We'll just have a quick look. And you know what, if you don't like it, we'll get rid of it, though I do hope you like it. After all, it is my favorite piece."

The doubt returned. Audrey wanted him to see her as a new person, not as some specimen he kept locked away in a hidden room. She sat there, stuck between a desire to appease him and the will to preserve the small amount of dignity she'd regained over the last week.

"It's taken a lot of courage for me to reach this point. Please understand. As I said, if you don't like it, we'll do away with it together." He leaned across the bar and kissed her forehead, and it lingered there like a forever promise.

She followed him down a spiral staircase, the corkscrew effect causing her vision to swim out of tandem with her steps. She paused and braced herself, and watched Ryan's long fingers slide along the banister, the same way he might have done hundreds of times before.

"Give me a second," she said, taking care not to lose her footing.

He offered no indication that he'd heard her.

"Ryan," she called out.

"Yes?" he said, turning.

"Wait for me, please."

"Oh, sorry." He lent her a hand, then led her down the stairs.

The studio looked nothing like the messy lair she'd imagined, at least from her elevated position on the stairs. The walls coming into view were a pleasing gallery gray, the lighting warm and inviting, and the air smelled fresh, as though the room underwent regular cleanings. The cooler air acted like a cold compress against her forehead. Maybe she'd made much ado about nothing.

But when stepped onto level ground she had to hold back a gasp. The large-scale images that covered almost every square inch of space told her she'd just stepped into a subterranean prison, where countless nude women trapped inside grainy, underexposed black and white images had been forced to stare at each other from across the room. Whether hollow, beguiling, or defiant, their eyes followed Audrey around the space, daring her to look between their legs. Every variety of female genitalia lay exposed on the wall, and the breadth of Ryan's obsession became clear.

"I could never do anything with them in the legitimate art world, of course. I'd be branded as just another pornographer. You know, perpetuating stereotypes and all that. It doesn't matter."

"Why?" she asked, gazing into the eyes of his subjects, all of them trapped in unique settings, but similar depraved circumstances when the shots had been taken.

"Why? I don't know. I suppose men never really had the right, which is fair."

"No, why do you do this?"

"Oh. *That* why. I've been searching for someone, really, someone like you who might understand me, who wouldn't judge me. Someone who could even... well, someone who could appreciate me, despite my flaws." He embraced her from behind. "I trust you, Audrey."

She turned and searched his eyes for telltale signs of insincerity. They shone blue and true, but frightened; the same look she'd seen on him the night of the blackout.

"And here it is," he said, leading her toward a large piece holding court in the center of the wall. And there sat Audrey, goddess of the damned, hanging at eye level with her legs parted, and staring into the lens (at herself, in this case) with a hazy kind of need—just a hopeless, anonymous creature lost in a world of apparitions.

This isn't me, she thought. How many women had he brought down here? How many had seen the truth of who they were in his eyes?

"You don't approve," he said, his voice softening.

"I'm trying to see the art in all this, but I don't belong up there. I don't want to be up there with the rest of them. I want… I *need* you to see me differently." She hated using that word, but it came out without her permission.

"I do. I swear I do," he said. "I did the moment you opened your door to me, though I tried my best to hide it. If you want me to take it down, I'll take it down. I'll take them all down, but I need to know how you feel about me," he said, drawing closer to her once more. "I need to know what's in your heart. Your secret heart; the one you've hidden from everyone else."

"I want to say it, but I'm afraid," she whispered.

"So am I, and before I do, I have one more thing to show you."

"What else is there?" she asked, the first tremor of fear coming as an unpleasant surprise.

He caressed her cheek with trembling fingers. "I trust you." With that he turned and disappeared into a small darkroom behind the stairway. A shape bathed in red light turned and offered her a tortured smile, then closed the door.

Alone with her thoughts, alone with the women, she considered going back upstairs, where they could communicate without all those prying eyes around them. This wasn't the place for vows and confessions of love. No amount of booze or proclamations of trust could change that.

She placed her foot on the first step, but a photo on the wall to her left stopped her cold. She leaned into the four-by-six-inch image and looked closer, confirming a nauseating suspicion. There sat Joy, legs parted, the photograph itself executed in the same crude, underexposed fashion like the others. But it seemed Ryan had added an additional detail by hand. He'd darkened Joy's eyes with a marker, so that she resembled a soulless creature, a succubus. Then Audrey recalled what Ryan had said about her eyes, about her being a young soul, and how she didn't recognize the futility of... the futility of *living*. Had he achieved the effect her eyes lacked by blackening them out?

Then Joy's video rushed back to memory, along with the desperation in her friend's voice, and the promise of love that turned to hate.

Audrey's heart raced ahead of itself. Logic did a somersault, and landed on its head. She glanced over her shoulder, removed her cell phone from her clutch, and dialed Joy's number. She needed to hear Joy's voice. A single reassuring word to set her more at ease. Instead, a familiar vibration and cheery jingling of bells rang out from within the studio. Audrey knew that sound. It reminded her of puffy white clouds and a smiling sun. It was Joy's ring tone.

Every hair on her body rose against the soft fabric of her dress. Her mouth went dry and her throat constricted. She traced the call to a worktable in the corner of the room, raced toward it, and zeroed in on the sound. The ringing continued in a cabinet below the worktable, like a cricket chirping in the dark.

She pulled on the latch with a shaking hand. Locked.

Then the chiming ceased and her call went to Joy's voicemail.

"Hey, what up? Please don't leave a message."

Audrey heard her own wavering breath recorded onto the device, then thought to say something. "Where are you?" she whispered, but the question fell on dead air.

She hung up, then stood on shaking legs to leave, but then the darkroom door creaked open, and a triangle of red light widened across the floor. Ryan, awash in a crimson haze, stepped through it and stood there in the nude, his expression twisted, tears on the cusp of falling from his eyes. Audrey quelled her reaction as best she could, but the sight of him in this condition rattled her to the bone. He stepped closer, and into more natural light, never breaking eye contact, and then his tears came down in a torrent, but no sound escaped his mouth. The juxtaposition disturbed her, but the sight between his legs terrified her.

His genitalia had been carved away. Deep scars ran from his lower abdomen to his inner thighs, as though a clawed beast had dug between his legs in pursuit of prey. What little of his manhood remained consisted of a misshapen tuft of hair and tattered folds of darkened, distorted flesh. She covered her mouth and fought to contain her tears.

Ryan turned sullen, as the women on the wall behind him stared and stared—his concubines, rising to his defense. "Please," he whispered.

She didn't mean to back away, to break his heart more than it had already been broken, but too much had happened too fast.

His expression turned dark, menacing. "No," he yelled. "No, no, no!" His face contorted to a monstrous mask, and the rest came out in a slobbering, tear-drenched stream. "You don't get to judge me. You, the lowest of the low. You, the embodiment of filth, the used up and the useless. *You* don't get to judge *me!*"

He continued toward her, his lean, muscular limbs twitching with every step, the tattered flesh between his legs flapping around.

"I'm not..." What had she meant to say? And why did her voice sound as though she were speaking through water?

"Why do you back away? I'm not a fucking monster. I have love in my heart, more love than you can imagine. I love you. Don't you understand that I love you?"

"I'm sorry," she managed to say, but fear had rendered her voice and limbs weak. Rather than attempting to get away, she chose to stay, to prove that she could move beyond her fear and show him some kindness and comfort. This wasn't calculated, but instinctive. She wanted to live, and sensed that he could snatch her life away if she said or did anything to upset him further.

A fresh bout of sobs dropped him to his knees, the pain in each heave almost grotesque, but it roused her pity. She went to him, grasped his hands, then intertwined her fingers through his. And Ryan's eyes, those perfect blue eyes, damaged beyond repair from the inside, found hers. Behind them stood the child to whom someone had done this terrible thing.

She said, "I do love—"

He grasped her throat before she could finish, and pressed his thumbs deep into her larynx, tighter, tighter, his teeth gritting with the effort. She pulled at his wrists, but his muscles had been forged in the gym over many years, it seemed, and his arms wouldn't budge.

Then he pushed her back, slamming her head hard against the cement floor. The pain shot down her spine, and along the backs of her legs. The lights in the room flickered, or maybe her sight had flickered. She couldn't tell which. She stole a saving breath, then found herself beneath him. He pressed harder and harder, his sobs straining through his throat. Lights twinkled on the outside edges of her vision, where the women observed with mild interest. His tears fell onto her face, her lips. She tasted the salty hemlock of pure suffering.

The child in him raged with a man's brute strength. She flailed and kicked, but his body contained the weight every man who'd ever been on top of her. He succeeded in sealing off her airway, and then she knew.

The end.

There.

Now.

But no, she still had the razor.

The razor.

She fought off encroaching darkness and felt around on the floor for her clutch. There, by his knee, a discarded thing that now seemed crucial. She got the clutch open and grasped the razor, still wrapped in tissue and useless. She felt her body drift above the floor somehow, but managed to shake the blade free. She gripped it as tight as she could, and slashed upward with all her remaining strength.

But she'd missed her mark.

Accept it. Fall into the darkness.

But then his grip slackened, and the deluge followed, hot and metallic. It spilled onto her face and chest, and left a crimson stripe down the middle of her dress when he stood up and backed away. Blood spurted between his clasped fingers with shocking force, drizzling to the floor in strings of rich syrup. Wide-eyed and confused, he garbled and gagged, then stumbled over his own feet, and crashed backward against the wall. Several photos came down with him in a rain of broken glass, no doubt adding to his injuries.

Audrey's body shook with adrenaline. She had trouble drawing in a breath, but then the first came, and then the next, and the next after that, until she felt well enough to stand. But when she got to her feet, she almost fainted. She stood there, teetering on the edge of darkness, the blade still warm and sticky in her hand. Then the sensation passed, leaving her aware of all that had happened.

Ryan wilted forward, and watched the blood cascade down his chest, between his legs, and onto the floor with dull fascination. A crimson pool spread outward from between his parted legs: castration and menstruation, united by the most unforeseeable circumstances.

She'd done this to him: opened him, silenced him.

Rather than leaving Ryan to bleed out his final moments alone, she approached, kneeled down into his blood, and pressed her hands against his wound to stem the flow, but she couldn't save him. The dam had burst. His rueful eyes slipped in and out of consciousness, and then a subtle change occurred. The rage behind them softened to something like sorrow, and then to peace, as though some malevolent spirit had fled its dying host. His complexion acquired a cadaverous pall. Then his eyes lolled upwards and found hers. They said, "I've been a bad boy, haven't I?"

Before the light of his being faded out, Ryan managed to smile. It was the most pathetic smile she'd ever seen.

Becoming a prostitute had been a natural progression of the downward slide; becoming a person not defined by her past took work, and she suspected the job would never be finished. After the police investigation and hearing, the annoying barrage of media inquiries, the persistent nightmares, the counseling sessions, and the six-month period of self-imposed exile, she managed to begin anew in a town far from Los Angeles, where the cost of living wasn't so unforgiving, and where people nodded and waved as they passed each other on the street.

Of the ninety-eight women Ryan had photographed, three

were cold-case homicides now solved, and nine were listed as missing persons, Joy included among them; and until they found her body, Audrey sensed there'd be no true closure. The authorities could only speculate on a handful of others. Whenever she replayed the events leading up to that horrific evening, she was astounded to discover the number of warning signs she'd ignored. She punished herself for it every day like a flogging ritual, but over time she came to the understanding that she was human and fallible, just like everyone else.

Reinvention also meant a job. A normal job.

Audrey tied the apron behind her waist, then tied her shoulder-length, chestnut brown hair into a ponytail. The after-church crowd had packed the diner to the rafters, and she knew her feet would see some serious mileage that day. Though she found the first few weeks on the job humbling (her moody manager enjoyed wielding meaningless power over her, and the pay was far below what she'd earned in her previous life), she now moved through the day with a kind of ease. She took customers' orders and refilled their coffee cups without complaint. She smiled at them and meant it when she removed their plates and asked if they wanted anything else. She'd earned the right to live a mundane existence, and had learned to find satisfaction in simpler pleasures. And no one knew, not a soul, that the cute young server who brought them their checks and told them to have a wonderful day had ventured through Hell and emerged a whole person.

Yet there were days—just a handful of them—when loneliness crept up behind her and whispered in her ear, and she'd once again find herself reaching for the letters Ryan had written to her. In those private, fragile moments she'd imagine him whole and alive, and it would reignite those first unwelcome pangs of love she'd felt for him.

She'd put the letters away, vowing to never open them again, then cuddle up with Charley, her adopted cat, and watch

TV. After six such broken promises, she went out to the enclosed patio and put the letters on a tabletop barbeque grill, doused them with lighter fluid, and lit a match. She hesitated, her eyes taking in Ryan's fevered sentiments one last time, until the little flame crept toward her fingertips. She dropped it onto the pages and watched them darken and curl in the tiny blaze. Tendrils of smoke rose upward, and she found it beautiful, like a freed spirit taking flight.

BLOOD LIKE DARK CHOCOLATE

She feasted at night
At Oxford
At Cambridge
At Bristol, Edinburgh, and Leeds
Always selecting daisy-fresh undergraduates
Drawing them from the crowd
Or from darkened corridors between buildings
With a flash of silver-green eyes

And they came, willingly
Wilting to her touch
Necks stretched backward, eyes to the stars
Their carotid arteries pulsating in time with her heart
As she drained them of their dreams
Dreams drenched in so much hope, so much innocence
That it helped her to remember the sweetness of life
Before the centuries
Before the fiend lured her into the cold night air, and said:

"Your life will stretch wider than the ocean, girl."

And on rare nights when she got her fill
Of youthful ambition and yearning
She would find herself craving, in the waning hours
before dawn
Something darker, something richer
A professor or two
Observed at a temporal distance for fifty years or more
Until they shuffled onto campus in tweed
Their faces grim with accumulated knowledge
Their daily routines repeating, repeating

And oh, how they turned from the coat rack
Or from the chalkboard
Or from the pages of some dusty old tome with a look of
mortal fear
That quickly melted to relief, then desire
They too wanted a taste of youth
To touch radiant skin unsullied by time
To run their arthritic fingers through hair finer than spun silk

She allowed them this small pleasure, employing no tricks
And when she invited them into her arms
They wilted, and wept

ALONG CAME THE FLIES

She wove a big web in the corner of the room
Up high
It looked like a piece of art
And when her guests arrived
They swarmed around the liquor cabinet like flies
Never thinking to look up
At the woman in black lace
Crouching at the center of her web
Fingers to the lines
Waiting for the slightest disturbance

UNFLAPPABLE

She turned before the clouded mirror wrapped in a gown of
wings,
Daring to indulge in memories
Of casting shadows on the moon,
Of tasting the cold, thin air at high altitude,
Of reaching the exalted moment—

A disembodied feeling at the edge of orbit,
The cosmos and all its secrets within her grasp;
Then, at the apex of creation...
...bending toward the earth

Down, down, through crystalline clouds,
A geometric constellation of city lights appearing below, then
Treetops and power lines,
And the lonely soul on a midnight stroll,
His life snatched away between two thoughts
And a breath.

She remembered landing on the deck of a sea-tossed ship,

And dispatching the entire crew,
Or flying across foreign lands,
Devouring armies, man-by-man.
She once hunted in Galilee,
In the time of Christ,
Collecting disciples like lambs,
Lifting them above the clouds,
Where she drained them, and dropped them.

Now, standing in cameo before the old mirror
She raised her chin and unfurled her wings—
Tattered, moth-eaten things,
Mere decorations.
Her eyes welled, but she shed no tears,
Taking some comfort in a lithe body,
Relatively untouched by time.
Flightless; yes, but she never wanted for nourishment.

Downstairs her victim waited in the parlor:
Another broken man, seeking a miraculous end to a broken life.
And as she descended the stairs, slowly,
The slumped, sallow figure holding his hat between his knees
Looked up and caught his breath.

COMMUNION

ONCE AGAIN, Batinah had seen the goddess, the hill, and the congregation of women, and had come to equate the emotions attached to these dream images with salvation.

She stared into the darkness as her husband, whose bulk had created a sinkhole at the center of the flimsy mattress, snored like a goat. Freedom from the bearded overlord seemed a terrifying prospect, but she could no longer ignore the message she'd received, so she slipped out of bed, packed her belongings—modest as they were—and started walking.

For three days and nights Batinah travelled alone on foot through the desert, keeping transient company with faster-moving phantoms in colored robes. It appeared these other women had all answered the same mysterious call, moving in the same direction with nothing but intuition to guide them. Batinah traded dried figs for clean water with a woman who'd wisely brought an abundance of it, and on the third night she shared a fire with twin sisters, who were thirty years younger than Batinah's sixty. Together, they passed the star-filled evening lamenting the difficulties of life in their respective villages, and the punishments they hoped to avoid when they returned to them, *if* they returned. The sisters sought a cure for river blindness, the onset of which had begun to turn their dark eyes an unearthly, mottled blue.

"We seem to share everything," one of them had said.

Rising beneath a blanket of pale stars, the fire beside her reduced to glowing embers, Batinah found herself alone once more. People had been kind, but they wouldn't wait for a woman who waddled along on a pair of sore, sandaled feet. She made a small breakfast of flatbread, dates, and tea, rolled up her bedding, then lumbered toward the first hint of light on the horizon.

The barren landscape offered no respite from the sun, and by the time it crested the distant hills it set her yellow robe aflame. She rested beside a rock that looked like a toy some giant child had left behind, and in the distance, she saw the line of people—a long, colorful snake from her perspective, winding up the hillside. At the hill's apex, and no larger than a pebble from her perspective, stood a crimson tent. The whole image wavered in the heat. At last, she was near, but relief arrived prematurely. Another hour passed before she reached the tail of the line, and seeing its true length up close came like a knife to the heart. She looked over her shoulder and saw a landscape devoid of people. The merciless sun had turned the ground into a sea of liquid mercury.

Batinah was the last to arrive.

Most of the women had taken to scooting forward from a seated position, rather than standing and taking the two or three steps necessary to keep the line moving. Batinah would not sit, however. If she sat, she might not have the strength to rise again, and what if it suddenly moved faster? She wanted to be ready.

"Rest your bones, dear," said the dark, wrinkled face peering up at her through a dusty black veil. "You're making me nervous."

Batinah ignored the old woman and counted the number of people ahead of her, but it soon became an impossible task, and her hopes dwindled. The seamless row of weary travelers burdened with bedrolls, gifts, and just enough food and water to sustain them stretched over a mile uphill. There would be no miracles left to divvy out by the time she reached the tent's entrance, she thought; nothing left to ease the pain of her difficult journey, or to soothe her troubled heart. She recognized some of the women ahead of her. One had offered her words of encouragement, and another had carried Batinah's pack a mile or so, but these other women now clung to their positions in line—and to their charity, it seemed—with prudence. Maybe exhaustion had gotten the better of them.

"You may as well sit," the old woman said.

Halfway up the hill, a woman in black wailed, her sobs and cries turning countless heads in that direction. Some rose to confirm with their eyes what their ears told them, and Batinah, who had nothing to lose by doing so, stepped away from the line to get a better look. Age had dulled her vision, and the heat lent an ephemeral quality to the figures in the distance, yet through these twin layers of diffusion she spied a woman clutching a makeshift stretcher that another woman—this one taller and draped in blue—dragged away from the line. The stretcher contained a small, limp body, and the grief-stricken woman in black fell to her knees before it. She then looked toward the heavens and screamed.

"The girl has died," the old woman said. "It isn't fair. We've had our time, but the child's life had just begun."

After what seemed a windswept eternity, the two women began their descent, dragging the child's lifeless body behind them, and those assembled on the hillside rose as they passed, bowing and offering blessings and prayers. The mourners neared Batinah, and she saw the suffering of the world behind their eyes. They had laid a thin blanket over the child's body, but her arm had slipped out from beneath it, and now dangled over the edge of the stretcher, tracing a small line in the dirt as they pulled her along.

"My heart is your heart," Batinah said, but they continued on without looking at her, and the line moved forward.

By mid-day, with the sun beating down upon her, she abandoned her standing vigil and inched along on her bottom like everyone else. Every so often a great commotion would rise from within the tent, as though a celebratory miracle had just taken place. It came again, and news of the event travelled down the line like slow-moving electricity, vivifying everyone it touched. A woman's sight had been restored, they said, and Batinah wondered if one of the twins she'd met the previous night got her wish. Some debated as to whether any of them at the back of the line would be so fortunate. With a mixture of amazement and dread, Batinah watched a dozen or so of the women who'd held communion inside the tent return back downhill. One of the them threw modesty to the wind and danced her way down on a pair of legs that had previously been bent and useless, with many in line cheering her on. Others returned silent and broken, and Batinah assumed these unfortunate women were beyond hope.

She opened her pack, spread a white cloth onto the ground, and began taking account of the offerings she'd brought on the journey. On it she placed a set of teacups, a broken necklace, and a hand-made doll dressed in silk robes. She then laid out a collection of spices, a pouch containing a rich, expensive tea she'd sworn not to drink unless there was nothing else at hand, and a small, silver coin. All these objects held both precious and practical value. The coin alone represented two weeks' nourishment. She counted the items, fifteen in all, then looked at the fifteen people ahead of her. Perhaps she could trade her way forward, but then that would leave nothing for her to offer in exchange for the miracle she sought.

The miracle.

Batinah had long kept a secret in her heart, a terrible secret that seemed determined to claw its way out of the graveyard of her childhood memories. In them, she saw a young, belligerent soldier pointing a rifle at her chest, shouting at her to provide him with a name. Others from the village stood beside young Batinah, their heads lowered, some of them crying. They'd been removed from their homes, were beaten and bullied, and seemed resolved to the notion that the soldiers would execute them if Batinah said the wrong thing. Their fates now lay in the hands of a nine-year-old girl.

She stopped herself from recalling the memory in full, and teardrops dotted the cloth spread out before her. In minutes, the sun stole them. Who was she to have come all this way seeking peace of mind, when so many others had come laden with more serious, debilitating ailments? An old woman with a troubled heart: they'd laugh her out of the tent. Hadn't she just witnessed the death of a child? What additional proof did she need that her request was selfish and small? After all, she'd lived all these years without telling anyone her story, and there were fleeting moments of happiness within that time, when the nightmares seemed to abate, and when she found enough work to distract her from the past. She would not barter for a better place in line; in fact, it was time to go, but rather than packing up her belongings and returning home with them to face her husband's wrath, she ambled toward the woman fifteen places ahead of her and handed her the necklace. Receiving it, the woman smiled with two rows of broken yellow teeth.

"I hope this earns you favor," Batinah said.

"Hope is all we have," the woman replied. She looked like a sun-scorched skeleton, and her dark eyes seemed too large for her skull. With frail hands, she tucked the necklace beneath her indigo robe.

All down the line Batinah went, offering a single gift and a blessing to each person, until she reached the old woman. She held out the coin. "This is for you. I cannot stay. I don't deserve to stay."

The old woman refrained from reaching for the coin. Instead, she gazed into Batinah's eyes and said, "If you were willing to risk your life to be here, then you deserve to stay. We all have our reasons, don't we? It's not for us to judge one reason against the next. And besides, I don't want to be the last person in line, so sit down and keep me company."

Minutes later, the line moved faster. Batinah took the old woman by the arm, and together they trudged upward, as the sun dipped behind them and stretched out their shadows. The climb proved far more difficult than Batinah had anticipated, but a chorus of voices from atop the hill, as well as an occasional swell of joyful cries from within the tent, released hidden reserves of energy in her legs. Their hands held outward for support, they negotiated a narrow crag in the escarpment and arrived at the plateau, and Batinah, lifting herself upright on shaky limbs, her lungs near to bursting, stood there in a state of awe.

Thousands of women milled about them. Many had already made camp, and were sitting around small fires boiling tea, or shaking the dust from their blankets. Some rested, while others sang and clapped in large groups, welcoming the evening's first stars. She'd never seen anything like it, nor had she ever fathomed that something like this was possible. Spread out along the perimeter, their eyes fixed on the horizon in all directions, were women in red robes, each with long rifles slung over their shoulders. They looked beautiful, their long hair dancing freely in the wind that rushed up over the steep embankment. *The Guardians.* She didn't know if they went by such a name, but it was the name her intuition provided. To her right stood a stable of Arabian horses that nickered and stamped, as their caretakers brought them bundles of barley hay and baskets filled with dates. But what captured her attention more than anything was the tent. It was larger than any dwelling she'd ever seen, it's walls undulating like swells on a blood red ocean.

The old woman turned toward Batinah and removed her veil, her eyes filling with tears. They embraced. Regardless of what happened inside the tent, Batinah had already found her miracle. She'd found it in the fortitude and determination of the woman in her arms, the scent of spiced delicacies lingering in the air, and in the sound of all those voices, singing and laughing, speaking the secret language of liberation.

"There's a chance we'll see her," the old woman said.

"I hope so," Batinah answered. "I know that I saw her in my dream, but I couldn't tell you what she looks like."

"I just saw the tent, but I knew she was inside, waiting for us all."

The entrance loomed closer, but as Batinah peered around the shoulders of those ahead of her, it became clear that there was another entrance on the opposite side of the tent, and another line of women stretching down the eastern side of the hill. Where had they all come from, and what had they endured along the way? More importantly, what had they left behind? Batinah imagined her husband rising the morning of her departure to find that breakfast hadn't been prepared, that the laundry hadn't been washed and hung out to dry, that the goats hadn't been milked, and that there was no one around to beat for it. Until that moment, she hadn't thought of him, as her entire will had been focused on reaching her destination. Batinah counted twenty people ahead of her, then fifteen. She knew this because the woman entering the tent was the same skeleton to whom she'd given the necklace.

"By her grace she shall be nourished," Batinah said.

"By her grace, indeed," the old woman replied.

Many women stood around the tent, drinking tea and talking to each other with animated gestures, as a group of children—girls all—raced around, whooping and hollering, kicking up tendrils of dust, and Batinah remembered that she'd once ran that way, except at the time she'd been running away from a bloody massacre.

"Get her!" came a voice from the past. She was once again inside the old village, weaving between ramshackle huts, nearly tripping, as the sound of heavy steps followed close behind; farther back, the sound of people begging for their lives. Then a hand tugged on her robe.

"Play with us," a smiling girl said to Batinah, who found herself once again in the present. The girl had taken her hand and was gently pulling on it. Her wide grin revealed the stubby beginnings of two adult front teeth.

"Later, I promise," Batinah said.

Another girl brought Batinah and the old woman cups of tea. After a few sips, Batinah's mood lightened. By her estimation, it would be nightfall by the time they reached the entrance, and though she hadn't planned for it, she now realized she'd be spending the night on the hilltop, and it doubled her excitement.

Suddenly the line moved forward with a rapidity she hadn't experienced all day, and the remaining group of people filtered in through the tent's opening. Inside, oil lamps hanging from the roof's wooden support beams burned brightly, and everywhere she looked she saw swaths of deep-hued silks, and ornate trays of burning incense that filled the air with calming aromas. Stacked near the wall to her left were countless leather bladders of water and sacks of rice. It was warmer inside the tent, and damp, due in part to the number of people occupying it. There were gentle murmurs, and a few in the crowd had dropped to their knees to pray. To her right stood a curtained room within the tent, where both lines now converged. The fabric in this smaller enclosure was sheer. Through it, Batinah saw a tall, graceful figure, perhaps the height of two men, seated atop some kind of pedestal, as several people on each side of it brought forth wet fabrics that they draped over its long arms.

"It's her," Batinah said to herself. "It's true. It's all true."

And though everyone now stood shoulder to shoulder, respect was given to the order they'd maintained outside the tent. I'm still the last, she thought. She'd come so far, had waited so long for this moment, that the urge to press forward seemed irresistible. A woman cried out from within the enclosure, as though the goddess had expelled a great pain from her body. Everyone pressed inward, tighter, tighter, and Batinah once again found herself beside the old woman, who took her hand.

One by one the people in front of them entered the enclosure. The giant woman behind it—no more than a ghostly impression from Batinah's perspective—looked weary. Her head, which appeared shaven, tilted forward, and her labored breath contained a deep, clicking sound. Shadow figures moved back and forth behind the enclosure, dunking and delivering soaked fabrics to others, who then draped them over the goddess's body. Like the perimeter outside, women in red guarded the entrance. One of them accepted the offerings each woman had brought, receiving them with a subtle bow, then placing them in a wheeled cart.

"What have you to offer?" the Guardian asked the old woman.

The old woman opened her palm, revealing a ring of the finest gold, the setting of which contained a radiant blue sapphire. The Guardian removed it from her hand as though she were picking a delicate bloom, then held it up toward a lamp to admire it. She then placed it atop an embroidered silk in the cart, as the second Guardian beckoned the old woman forward.

"Enter with a pure heart and a clear mind," she said, opening the curtain.

Batinah's heart nearly stopped. The goddess, who stood nude, except for the wet, blood-tinged cloths the assistants had draped over her body, lowered her gaze toward Batinah. The goddess's eyes were large and luminous, all-knowing. The old woman stepped inside, and the curtain closed.

"What have you to offer?" the Guardian asked Batinah.

Her memory faltered. What had she brought? Many things. Wait, she'd given them all away. Then she remembered the coin, and searched the familiar folds of her robe for it. "I had a coin," she said, still searching. She unfurled her bedding and a few bits of gravel fell out. "I must have lost it along the way. I know I had it. It was silver, and… I know I had it. I *know* it."

"You bring nothing?"

Batinah wanted to cry, but she held back her tears. Looking around, she saw that she was indeed the last woman in line, the last woman in line who had nothing to offer. She shook her head no.

"Then you are truly blessed," the Guardian said.

"Enter with a pure heart and a clear mind," the second Guardian said, opening the curtain.

Batinah stepped forward, giving herself body and soul to the moment. The pain in her feet disappeared, her worries about the coin fled, and the past and the future became harmless rumors. She'd entered that delirious middle world between dreams and reality, where neither held dominance, and a warmth unlike any she'd ever felt radiated from her center outward. With great effort, the goddess before her leaned upright with her long arms outstretched, and Batinah saw the fullness of her, the truth of her, the divine femininity she knew was stronger than steel. Attendants came to the goddess's aid, removing the damp cloths from her arms, shoulders, and legs. Her brown-blue skin bore countless, symmetrical cuts, and the surrounding tissue of each appeared raised and irritated. The reason for this became clear. The goddess's head and face were covered in large, pearlescent scales, but the entire region of her body below the neck looked as though it had been plucked, one scale at a time.

Batinah kneeled.

The goddess raised her head and opened her eyes. "Batinah," she said, accentuating each vowel with a voice several octaves lower than any man's, "the one who hides. Have you been hiding?"

"Yes," Batinah said.

"The one who hides in her captor's cruel embrace."

"Yes." The tears came and she wasn't ashamed.

"I know your story as well as my own. Nothing you could have said would have saved the people in your village. Poor child. You couldn't have stopped that soldier from taking you as his young bride. Even now, you cannot take back the innocence he stole from you, but you can take back the remainder of your life," she said, reaching toward her neck and removing a scale from it. "Partake of my body and be nourished."

Batinah opened her mouth and received the scale. It was hard as a fingernail at first, but sweet, and within seconds it began to soften and disintegrate in her mouth. Something also melted away within her. It could have been her thoughts, or her past, or the anguish she'd bottled and preserved for so many years. She wasn't sure which. She just knew that she felt lighter, stronger. The muscles in her face, which she never really knew she had, relaxed. Her shoulders softened, as her spine seemed to elongate and straighten; and the belief that she could say anything to anyone—something else she'd never known possible—asserted itself in her consciousness as a divine directive.

"I too must heal," the goddess said, as the attendants reappeared, putting ointment on her skin and draping her limbs once more with the wet fabrics. "Join the others and celebrate."

They led Batinah out of the tent, and before she realized it was all over, a group of young girls, the same ones she'd seen playing together earlier, approached and embraced her, then pulled her toward the celebration. The stars were more brilliant than ever—one for each soul, Batinah thought—and for the first time in fifty years she didn't feel alone. But she must find the old woman; must find her and thank her.

The foot came hard to Batinah's stomach, delivering her to a world of sunlit agony. After a moment of breathless shock and confusion, the room came into focus. She saw the rusted, corrugated metal walls of her dwelling, the little propane burner atop the crooked table, the bare dirt floor, and her husband's hairy, sandaled foot retracting from the kick.

"Get up, you cow," he said, kicking the bed's frame, then walking away.

She waited until he left the room, then swung her legs over the edge of the bed and sat up, groaning in pain. As it subsided, the old familiar hate returned. Worse, she'd been dreaming about something miraculous—a journey of some kind, and in it everything wrong about her life had been set right, though she couldn't quite remember how. There was an old woman, and a tent, and... the thread came apart, and all she was left with was the *feeling* of it, a feeling of freedom, power, and maybe forgiveness; not for her husband, of course, but for herself. She held onto it as long as she could, but in time routine swallowed her once more, and it soon became nothing more than a vague longing, then the memory of a memory, until one day the dream disappeared altogether.

Several years later, after the morning of her husband's burial, the women in her village swarmed her little house and filled it with food, drink, and conversation. They consoled her, though she needed no consolation, and promised to keep better company. One of them brought a dessert of hardened sweet-bread, and tasting it, the dream came back to Batinah with shocking clarity, and in that moment, she realized the goddess lived inside all of them. They gave to their husbands, they fed their children, becoming monastic masters of self-denial in the process, and the demands of it required healing. Batinah then told them the story of how she'd come to live in their village, how her husband had once been a soldier, and that he'd raped her when she was just nine years old, as his comrades laid waste to her village and the people in it. She told them all of this as though she were reading them a series of facts from a history book, and when she finished, not a word was spoken. But something very important happened. At the age of sixty-four, Batinah's life finally began.

PREY ANIMAL

By a trick of accelerated devolution,
Norman's eyes shifted toward the sides of his head.
He'd eaten his Tuesday night meatloaf
(On a Wednesday, mind you)
woke the following morning feeling,
well...
...worse than usual, and a little disoriented,
then stumbled down the hall toward the restroom.

He looked in the bathroom mirror.
Turned his head side-to-side.
"Of course, this happened to me," he said, scrutinizing his new profile.
A lamb's eye stared back—oblong irises, pupils like long black pills.
"Oh dear," he said. "Oh dear, oh dear, oh... baa."

But having a prey animal's eyes had its benefits:
He could finally graze in relative peace,

his boss never again got the jump on him,
and he never had to look people in the eye.
He'd just smile and nod,
and think how wonderful it was
to see trouble coming from both directions.

PILLARS

Great pillars of flesh had arisen around the world—
first in Hollywood, then in Bollywood,
then in every other remaining territory named or unknown.

They all started innocently, just someone lying face down
on the pavement, in the dirt.
They always did it outdoors.
Another would come along and join the pile,
and so it went, without reason,
the pile growing apace to the number of people within sight
of it.

Soon those below were suffocated and crushed,
as newcomers clambered upward.

Anyone who tried to intervene was drawn into it,
accepting death face-down.

The highest pillar appeared in Shanghai—some fifty stories
tall,

a full city block at its base, its apex lost in the smog.
Aerial images shocked the world:
A sky teaming with gulls,
feasting at will, as climbers fought for purchase on a mountain
of pale,
bloated bodies.

Only the strongest, most determined climbers reached the top.

People watched pillars grow from their office windows,
and moments after seeing them, they went downstairs and
climbed.

Thus, buildings were drained and pillars erected.

People in the west attributed the height of Shanghai's pillar
to population density and collectivism.

But the U.S. had its own problems. People were told not to
venture outside, otherwise they'd risk being arrested. But there
weren't enough prisons for all of us,
and the pillars were plentiful.

JOY RIDE

LOBBYJAW SAT up in the bus stop bench, his stomach churning with excitement. "Skatch. Hey, Skatch. Here he comes!"

The ice cream truck rounded the corner at a crawl, its carrion call to the denizens of Hell's Fourth Circle warbling through a rusted megaphone speaker mounted to the top. It came in a cloud of flies. It came sputtering and spitting soot into the sky, the air warm, wet, and metallic after a recent drizzle of calves' blood. The city itself reminded Lobbyjaw of a used condom, everything sticky and stuck together and gagging on its own putrescence. Everything bathed in red. A diseased city, with banks of garbage lining the streets and climbing up the walls of buildings; all of it baking like a fetid soufflé beneath Hell's three suns.

Lobbyjaw felt itchy in his powder blue suit. He wanted to kill himself again, just for fun, and to escape the heat for a while, but then the ice cream truck arrived, right on time.

"Would you take a gander at that. Beeeeeautiful. Skatch. Hey, Skatch!"

Lobbyjaw turned and found Skatch throwing dice against the wall with three other hoodlums from the Fourth's lower east side. Skatch stood out among them, with his zoot suit, wallet chain, and big black pompadour crowning his handsome head. Skatch's thin mustache made him look like a connoisseur of ladies' legs, turtle soup, and champagne, none of which existed in abundance in the Fourth. You first had to find it, then fight over it. Skatch, he knew, always carried a switch blade for such occasions. Skatch, who'd died in the year 1954.

"Skatch. Get over here. Quick!"

Skatch scooped up his dice, collected his winnings, and bopped his way toward the bus stop, a whistle on his lips, a snap on his fingers. Skatch's scheming eyes widened when he caught sight of the ice cream truck. "Skip-skap, dooby-dap, skibby-dobby-do!"

"I know. I was trying to tell you, but you're over there jerkin' off with your dice."

Skatch put his foot on the bench, whipped out a long red rag, and buffed his shoes, his eyes never straying from the approaching truck.

It soon drew a small crowd, and Lobbyjaw stared and stared, dreaming not of the treats within, but of taking it for a spin. "What'd I tell ya? Ain't she beeeeautiful? Oh, what I wouldn't do with a truck like that. Where I wouldn't go. Who I wouldn't run over."

The truck's steel-grated service window slid open, and a fat man known as Harry Glum appeared behind it in a dingy white apron, his bald head almost blue with Thought Rot, and crowned with a tiny paper hat. When he spoke, he sounded as though he'd just entered puberty, his voice wavering between two octaves. "One at a time, everybody. One at a time."

"Boom-chika-cha?"

"Harry ain't got no shotgun. I guarantee it."

"Skiddly-boop?"

"Sure, I'm sure. I'm not saying he doesn't have a few tricks and traps in there, maybe even a stabby-stick or three, but a gun? No, Harry ain't got a gun." Lobbyjaw licked his lips. "Hey, I got an idea. Lend me a quarter."

Skatch reached deep into his pocket, then hesitated.

"I'll pay you back. C'mon, lend me quarter."

Skatch's pocket jingled as he removed a single, shiny quarter.

Lobbyjaw snatched it from his fingers. "Follow me."

He led Skatch scatting and bopping toward the crowd of eager customers, most of whom had taken to shoving and shouting, as they fought to get to the head of the line. Lobbyjaw knew crowds. Lobbyjaw knew lots of things. He knew how to press his short, stocky frame between people, elbows out, his voice booming, like he did now.

"What a day, what a day! So damn hot! Sure could use me a cool, tasty treat." Someone shoved him from behind. Turning, he said, "Back off, you dogs. Wait your turn. I'm a paying customer." He held the quarter high, showing it off.

The eyes of the crowd fell upon the coin, as if they'd never beheld a thing of such beauty. Quarters looked like full moons, after all—silver and round, with a little man in cameo on the surface, and since no one in the fourth had seen the moon since departing the earthly realm, passing through purgatory's processing unit and winding up here, they seemed to read something of feminine, mythological significance in George Washington's wig. A moon over Paris. A moon over Rome. A moon over the heads of the damned. Lobbyjaw waived it around, as though teasing a pack of hungry dogs with a treat, then threw it down the street. Off they went, all pratfalls and clumsy maneuvers as they chased the rolling coin toward a storm drain. It rolled out of reach, careening to the right as though waning, then down it went, into the wretched waters of the sewer. The undeterred members of the crowd reached in, cursing and fighting, tearing at each other's clothes and hair.

Those who remained claimed their spots behind Lobbyjaw and Skatch.

Lobbyjaw winked at his partner. "Ah, peace and quiet at last. "He then turned toward the ice cream truck's proprietor. "Harry, my good man, what's on the menu? You got tutti frutti?"

"No ice cream today. What you see is what I got, fellas," Harry said, adjusting his hat, then jabbing a stubby thumb toward the menu pasted on the side of the truck. Many of the items had been crossed out, and those that remained looked foul enough to curdle the milk in cow's teat.

"Oh, and what I fine selection you have," Lobbyjaw said in a refined manner, while eyeing pictures of rancid delights—fried monkey knuckles, popcorn flies, roach á la mode, rat tails and hot sauce (Zingers)... Nothing cool, nothing frozen, and the stench wafting from the window reminded him of the time he'd worked in the mausoleum brothels, cleaning the floors and ceilings with a mop.

"How much for the monkey knuckles?"

"Two bits."

"Two bits. Hmm. Two bits...." He nudged Skatch again, and gestured with his eyes toward Skatch's pocket. "Two bits, you say? Are they good? Are they delicious?"

"Fellas, I don't mean to brag or nothing, but I guarantee these here are the tastiest, most delectable, lip-smacking monkey knuckles you'll find in the Fourth."

"Mighty big claim, Harry. Mighty big claim." He nudged Skatch again, then whispered through the side of his mouth. "Two bits, on the double." Back to Harry. "I'll confess, you've piqued my curiosity. Tell you what, we'd like two orders of the knuckles, extra salt."

"Two knucks, double-salt, coming up," Harry said, turning to prepare the order. He removed the knuckles from a clear plastic bag smeared with grime, and dropped them in the fryer, the bubbling oil the color of tainted urine.

"Skodda-bodda-bing-bong," Skatch said under his breath.

"I know what I'm doing. Just lend me four bits and watch the master work. C'mon. Do you trust me?"

Skatch shrugged.

"What about the time I got in you in freebie-jeebie at the brothel? What about the time I got rid of the eel in your sink with a coat hanger? Remember that?"

In a scratchy voice, Skatch said, "Zip-bob-daddly-doop."

"No time to argue. Just—"

Harry returned to the counter as the knuckles bubbled in the fryer behind him. "That'll be four bits, fellas."

"Harry, old pal, I've been wondering. Is something wrong with your truck?"

"What do you mean?"

"It goes so slow. Slug slow. Grandma slow."

"I've gotta drive slow on account of customers."

"Sure, but what I mean is, does she have any goose in her step? Ever get her up two twenty? Thirty? Forty?"

"Gee, I don't know. I put my foot on the gas, she goes forward. I put my foot on the brake, she stops. I put her in reverse, she backs up. I flick that little switch over there by the dash board and she sings. She's a working truck, not a race car, by golly."

"What if you had to bug out? Could you get her up to sixty?"

Harry scratched his head, his thick lips pursed above a small chin. "I guess so."

"Hmm. Eighty?"

"Well, let's not get crazy, but I suppose."

A timer went *ding,* and Harry turned to retrieve the order.

"Four bits, Skatch, and follow my moves."

Skatch sighed, then reached into his pocket, searching by

feel alone for four quarters. The sound of fondled silver drew unwanted attention from the customers behind them.

No sooner than Skatch's hand appeared from his pocket, someone reached out and grabbed his wrist. Big mistake. In three rapid moves, Skatch produced a switch blade with his free hand, flicked it open, and shanked the would-be robber below the ribs. The man pulled away and fell face-forward, groaning and bleeding on the asphalt, as the others backed away. Skatch pounced, stabbing the backs of the man's thighs, his buttocks, his kidneys. He then found the bull's eye, and rammed the blade up the man's rectum. His victim squealed like a stuck pig, then found his footing and fled, clutching the seat of his pants as though he'd crapped out his intestines.

Skatch returned to the counter with a red-speckled grin, coins in hand. "Dooby-dat?"

"I saw! Nice work. He'll be regular for a month. Now, about them bits."

Skatch offered a look of warning before handing them over.

"You're a pal. A real pal. Now, follow my lead."

Lobbyjaw stood on the tips of his toes and looked inside the truck for signs of weaponry or trip wire explosives, but instead got a look into the dark regions of Harry's soul. He tugged on Skatch's sleeve and brought him closer to the counter.

"Look, look," he whispered, "Harry's a pre-vert." Along the back wall Harry had taped a collage of clothing advertisements for boys, some in swimsuits, some in their underwear. Below it lay a filthy, fold-out sofa. On the shelves next to it he spotted commercial-sized jugs of corn oil. "Harry's lube," he said, his eyes going to the fryer. He shivered in disgust.

He then whispered into Skatch's ear. Skatch nodded once, twice, a third time. They shook hands, and turned to face Harry, who slid two paper trays of monkey knuckles toward them. They looked like fried tarantulas, the grease drenching the paper.

"Hey, where'd everybody go?" Harry said, tilting back his hat and leaning out the window.

"Guess they lost their appetites. Four bits for the order, you said?"

"Gee, that's strange. Yeah, four bits, fellas."

Lobbyjaw jingled the coins in his palm, then held them just out of Harry's reach. He teased Harry's arm out farther. Harry grumbled, his tongue bitten in concentration, as he made the mistake of reaching out with his entire arm.

Lobbyjaw said, "Twenty-two skidoo!"

Skatch drew his knife, and Lobbyjaw grabbed Harry's arm, pulling it backwards against the counter. Before the panic reached Harry's face, Skatch started stabbing, stabbing, stabbing, as if to cut Harry's arm off at the elbow. He must have hit an artery, as Harry howled in agony; howled as though he'd never so much as stubbed his toe, neither in this life, nor the previous. The blood came thick and rich, gushing and spattering onto the laminated counter, its surface decorated with puffy white clouds and rainbows. More blood spurted into the trays of monkey knuckles, like ketchup.

Lobbyjaw pulled with all his might, hoping to yank Harry out the window and onto the street, but for all Harry's pudgy flesh, fear lent him the strength of a gorilla. All the while he swiped at something mounted above the window with his free hand. The hand returned holding a sawed-off shotgun. Lobbyjaw locked eyes with the barrel, then ducked.

BOOM!

"Go for the eyes, Skatch!"

Skatch contained Harry's shooting hand and stabbed the man's face, missing his right eye by inches. However, he put a hole through both sides of Harry's cheeks. Then, in a swift move, he wrested the shotgun from Harry's hand and threw it across the street, where it skidded and clacked against the curb.

All the while the Happy Ice Cream Day song jingle-jangled from the speaker.

"AHHH!" Harry gagged on his own blood, then bit down on the blade to prevent further assault, his twin rows of gapped teeth crunching metal. Skatch engaged him in a tug of war, cranking the treat vendor's head up and down, dislodging his paper hat. It caught an ill wind, and in a moment of carefree glee, Lobbyjaw followed its flight toward sewer, where the coin-chasers had turned toward the commotion transpiring by the truck. Seeing trouble afoot, or fun, they came running.

"Get him, Skatch. Hurry."

Zing. Skatch freed his blade, and this time his aim was true. "Ramma-lamma!" He drove the blade into Harry's eye socket, the sound clean and wet, the shriek from Harry's mouth guttural and rather sad, as the gelatinous mush of his eye dribbled down his cheek.

"That's it. Get the other one!"

But the encroaching crowd drowned out Lobbyjaw's cry for further violence with shouts of their own. Addicts, Lobbyjaw thought, in need of another fix of the caustic oil in Harry's fryers. He turned and hung with all his weight from Harry's extended forearm, the joints and tendons therein popping and snapping as he used the counter's edge for leverage. He kicked the first man that reached him with both legs, saying, "Do you know who I am? DO YOU KNOW WHO I AM! I'M JACOB T. LOBBYJAW, ESQUIRE!" Then, turning. "Finish him, Skatch."

Harry looked close to fainting, his face a mask blood, as Skatch went for his neck. Lobbyjaw had less than two seconds to admire Skatch's knifework before the crowd slammed into him, clawing at his eyes, punching him in the balls, the pain blinding. Still, Lobbyjaw clung to Harry's arm the way a monkey clings to a low-hanging branch, as a pride of hungry lions growled below. Harry's blood-slickened arm slipped from Lobbyjaw's grasp, and he fell on his ass. Then came the kicks to his face and chest. He raised his elbows to protect himself, and among a confusion of blurred feet and sticky soles, he spotted Skatch's polished shoes, all covered in Harry's blood. The shoes seemed to dance, then came the whistling, zipping sound of Skatch's blade. Skatch cut and sliced his way into the throng, driving Lobbyjaw's attackers back in shock and terror.

What a conquistador! Lobbyjaw thought, with renewed respect for his friend. Yes sir, a regular Don Juan Decaptitato. "That's it, Skatch! Give it to 'em good," Lobbyjaw said through swollen lips, the taste of blood in his mouth adding to the thrill of it all.

Their attackers retreated, most of them clutching their wounds and stumbling toward the curb to bleed in peace. Skatch claimed his ground with a grandiloquent stance, like some dapper toreador who'd bested a bull, though his pompadour had fallen from grace, his long bangs wet and stringy and covering his eyes, but still dashing, in a way. He whipped them back with a hand, and seemed to suck in the pomegranate essence of blood on his mustache.

"This is how we make many splendors among the peoples," he said.

Lobbyjaw's jaw dropped. He'd never heard Skatch say anything buy scatty-jazzy words, those zoops and sciddly-bops of which Lobbyjaw had learned to interpret over many years of bosom devilry.

"Heck, Skatch. That's a mouthful. You're a damn poet."

"Ratta-tatta, zatta-maca."

The truck lurched forward, breaking and charging in short bursts, as if Harry had forgotten how to drive.

"Quick, gimme me a boost!" Lobbyjaw got to his feet and gripped the counter, as the truck went back and forth, its gears grinding. He lifted a foot, and Skatch catapulted him through the service window and into Harry's kitchen area. The truck shifted to and fro, like a tug boat on choppy waters. Hot oil spilled from the fryers and onto the floor, searing the rubber mats there, as the Happy Ice Cream Day song wailed from the speakers. Lobbyjaw spotted Harry slumped over the wheel, grunting and groaning in agony.

Lobbyjaw looked around for a suitable weapon. Harry's cleavers and butcher knives hung from a magnetic rack above the food prep area, where many a dead and rotting thing lay, but Lobbyjaw took keener interest in the oil. He found a collection of coffee cans on a lower shelf, each one labeled by date on strips of masking tape. He peeled back a plastic lid and gagged. Harry, it seemed, liked to collect his spunk. Holding his nose, he lifted the can over the fryer. A congealed, cylindrical collection of Harry's man sauce slid into it, like expired cream of mushroom soup from a can. *Splorsh.*

Lobbyjaw waited, tapping his foot as the glob fried to a nice golden brown, and as Harry finally found first gear and put the truck into motion. He whistled, waiting, waiting. Done.

He removed the fryer basket and added an unhealthy portion of salt from a greasy tin shaker. He then crept toward the front of the truck, taking care not to slip in the slick mess dripping at his feet. He swung the basket all the way back, then... *whap!* A side order of hot crud across Harry's face.

Harry howled, his skin sizzling, his collected jizz still soft in the middle, and oozing down his apron. Harry lost control of the wheel and slammed into a parked car, throwing Lobbyjaw headlong into the windshield. Seconds later, with his ears ringing, Skatch appeared outside the driver side door window, pounding and hollering.

"Skit-skat-doodily-dap!"

BOOM!

Someone had found the shotgun. Buckshot went *ting, ting, ting* across metal, with an errant bit of buck shot cracking the sideview mirror.

"Momma!" Harry said, gurgling blood and mucus, and the

cooked contents of his baby-makers. "Momma, momma, momma…"

Lobbyjaw got the driver side door unlocked. No sooner, Skatch yanked it open.

"Sayonara, ya pre-vert," Lobbyjaw said, kicking Harry out of the vehicle. He waved for Skatch to get in. "C'mon, c'mon."

Skatch stepped on Harry's back, hopped in, and scooched over to the passenger seat.

Then came the exalted moment, as Lobbyjaw sat and put his hands on the wheel. No ship's captain, airline pilot, or bulldozer operator ever knew with such profundity the absolute power and authority Lobbyjaw felt while gripping the wheel, or so he believed. Only gods and aliens understood the glory of the wheel, piloting their mighty ships and saucers through the cosmos, the former looking for cities to raze, the latter for monkeys to raise in their likeness.

He put his hand on the gearshift knob, put the beast in reverse, and pressed the accelerator to the floor, swinging the behemoth into the center of the street. *Thud* went the sound of someone going under the wheels, followed by a scream, then a clump, clump, clump.

"One down."

He ground the gears, looking for first, which allowed some of Harry's uninjured supporters time to rally and charge toward the windshield, some wielding pipes, other rocks and bricks thrown with deadly accuracy. Through the grease-speckled windshield Lobbyjaw caught sight of a man limping toward them with Harry's shotgun in his hands. He raised the barrel and took aim.

"Duck!"

They dipped low, but no explosion followed. Lobbyjaw leaned up to see the amateur assassin inspecting his failed weapon in disappointment.

"You need bullets, jack ass!"

The man gave up trying to solve the problem, then wielded the gun like a truncheon and charged, his battle cry drawing a wheeze of laughter from Lobbyjaw.

He turned toward Skatch, "Ready to have some fun?"

"Ratta-chatta."

"You said it."

Lobbyjaw put the truck in first gear, then floored it. He shifted into second, third, the speedometer's needle twitching as it climbed to ten, twenty, thirty mph. Those who'd attempted to oust Lobbyjaw and Skatch from Harry's truck turned tail and ran, but he'd already closed the gap between them. His nearest target turned in terror, and in a moment of sublime malevolence, Lobbyjaw slammed into him, the sound of flesh on metal sweeter than the performative moans of whores, whose rooms he once cleaned for a pittance, and an occasional hand job. Darker days. Sadder days. Day's he'd left behind. And now, men fleeing in fright before him, their slow feet promising cruel delights.

"Woo-hoo!"

Clump, clump, clump. Down the runners went, screaming, their heads and bones popping and snapping beneath the wheels. They'd soon wake in Purgatory's vast, fluorescent-lit lobby, its cubicles filled with the vilest, drowsiest, most complacent administrators in the known universe, its waiting areas and hallways packed full of sorry sods and hopeless sinners, some of whom had fallen beneath the wheels of Harry's truck. Perhaps the people he'd killed would get assigned to new circles, assuming they'd learned a few lessons while sweating out their days in the Fourth.

Not that it mattered to Lobbyjaw, who watched in amazement as the speedometer climbed to forty mph, then fifty, everything inside the stinking truck rattling and shaking—utensils, pots and pans, and cans of Harry's cum. He beamed at the sight of the fuel gauge: a full tank of go get 'em. Better yet, plenty of people to ram on the road ahead.

"Hey, that was worth four bits, wasn't it?"

Skatch cleaned his blade with the same rag he'd used to polish his shoes, and said, "Skoddy-bompa-do."

"Okay, okay. Five bits, but who's counting? Anyway, what did I say, huh? I said stick with me and you'll go places. Well, ain't we going places? In fact, where *do* you wanna go? Just name it, pal. You earned it."

Skatch blew fog on his blade, then polished it to an icy shimmer. Finally, after a fair amount of steely-eyed rumination, he unglued his reflected gaze from its surface, and said: "Compadre, I want to go to a place where the moon shines like a quarter in the sky, and where the stars drift in the heavens, as if borne upon a gentle breeze. I want to go where the women are beautiful and clean, their lips sweeter than powdered sugar. I want to see marble fountains and great pillars reaching to the clouds. I want to go where people sing songs of joy, and where no one curses or does unpleasant things to one another. I want to go where the light of truth shines brightly in every heart, every soul. But mostly, amigo, I want to see my sweet mother, Yessenia."

Lobbyjaw subdued the urge to laugh at his friend's ridiculous fantasy. "You mean..." Lobbyjaw pointed upward, toward Heaven.

Skatch nodded. "But please, do not ask me for any more money. Money between friends is... well, it can cause rather unpleasant complications, yes?" Skatch tested the sharpness of his blade against his thumbnail, and cut off a sliver so thin that it took flight and drifted around in the cab.

"No more mula. Got it. So, Heaven?"

"Why not? I hear it is nice."

"I love your attitude, Skatch. Love it! And you're right: why not? But if we're gonna get there, I'd better turn this beast around."

"You know the way?"

"The way I see it, we're headed downward, toward The Fifth. Stands to reason The Third's in the opposite direction, then The Second, then The First. And then..."

Lobbyjaw imagined crashing through Purgatory's glass doors, and mowing down all the bloodless bureaucrats occupying those squeaking chairs and faux wood desks; then, should Hell's three suns shine upon his pimpled bottom, the gates of Heaven. He and his stinking, diseased ice cream truck, packed full o' sin, ramrodding its way into through God's courtyards and golf courses, and mowing down dopey people dressed in matching white polo shirts and khakis. He'd drive it right into God's throne room, stop, and rev the engine, daring his bearded maker to make the first move. Good times ahead, he thought. Damn good times.

"Hey Skatch," he said, turning the truck around.

"Yes, compadre?"

"I got me an idea."

CROW

Garroter crow
Mr. Black
Keeper of dreams
Please come back
I'll never ask you to sing, my friend
Never ask you to sing
And nevermore will I implore
A single day of spring

BIG ORANGE MOON

The old man hated Halloween
Hated kids coming to his door
Ringing the bell, knocking
Even though he turned out all the lights

He lived alone
Never had children of his own
And when the children haunted the sidewalks
Kicking leaves and laughing

Screeching, screaming
Running, dashing
Into dappled shadow
He would turn from the peephole, saddened

Too many lost Octobers
Too many nights without magic
Too many years between
Abandoned dreams and the grave

Until tonight, until the change
That started with a gentle knock
Drawing him to the door
To the peephole, glowing orange

No one on the porch, but there
Hanging above the treetops
A big orange moon, wider than a city block
Cresting the rooftops

A moon to rouse an old man from his dreads
And when he stepped out to greet it
He found himself running like a child of ten
Faster, faster, like a werewolf among friends

BEHIND CLOSED DOORS

Behind closed doors
They called him fragile
Sure to fly away in a breeze

Behind closed doors
They called him sickly
Sure to die from a sneeze

From a bee sting, the needle
A scraped knee
The measles

And behind a closed door
He listened and sighed
Mixing their poison by fireside

WHEN IT TAKES YOU

Do you sink into a cool black pool,
Or rise to a golden kingdom
To admire without self-recrimination
The great truths of your time?

Do you stroll through a warehouse of your regrets,
Like some curator of a museum that never opens,
Or do you simply turn off the lights
And walk away?

Do you panic, do you pray?
Some say you find peace in your final moments,
The result of your brain releasing dopamine
That it held like a secret stash all through the years

It knows, it knows
It throws you a party

But then, how does it know?

OLD DREAD NO. 9

ONCE UPON A DARKER TIME, my dear friend discovered the Old Dread No. 9, and once tasted, the tonic took control of his life for nearly a decade, until the night it led him nude and raving to a place few knew existed, and fewer still had entered.

It's a horrible thing to witness, even in your most despised enemies, never mind in someone you might call brother, and for whom you'd forsake your own soul to save. But there's no saving the person who finds in that odious black bottle a kind of sanguine euphoria, a release from the tyranny of inhibition, and a feeling of creative conquest known only to the greats. I know you won't heed my warning, you poets, painters, and musicians, but beware! Some doorways in the mind are better left locked, some visions better left unwitnessed. In short: If you get hooked on that purple-black bracer, which does not taste like licorice liqueur, but rather blueberries distilled in vats of angels' spit and moonlight, then you're *doomed.*

Utterly.

The substance, you see, slithers into the mind with liquid tentacles, teasing pleasure receptors like an expert lover, while putting a stranglehold on the prefrontal cortex, where better sense and self-preservation reside, turning otherwise upright people into hunched philanderers, petty thieves, violent, self-loathing addicts, and wreckers of dreams.

It blackens the rose and darkens the sky; it kills all hope and X's the eyes. It goes by the names Inamorata and Libertine, Lollygag and Stag, but let's call it by its true name: Old Dread No. 9. Not five, six, seven, or eight, but *nine,* as in Dante's nine levels of Hell; as in nine lives of a cat—a black one, born on the thirteenth hour of the thirteenth day of the thirteenth month.

And if you want a better metaphor, you're out of luck. All this to say those who imbibe are in for the nine-year ride of their lives, assuming they don't keel over beforehand in a puddle of their own making, or cut their lives short by rope, pistol, or knife. Those who do make it to the other side—yes, the other side, as I've seen it firsthand—forfeit all they ever were or would ever become for the chance to live out their wildest fantasies among their own kind.

I'm sure you're familiar with the story of Mort Gallagher, the famous jazz musician who disappeared without a trace after a nine-year ascent to stardom. I happen to know where he went (well, I have a theory, anyway), and only for the purpose of drawing a comparison between Mort's fate and my friend's, will I share a portion of the banjo player's tale, which I've studied in great detail.

In the first quarter of the 20th century, young Mort chicken-picked his way off the farm and found himself busking on busy street corners in Chicago, his tin cup filling up fast, for his fingers moved with such precision and speed, such joyful musicality, that passersby felt obliged to reach in their pockets and toss him a dime or two, sometimes a quarter.

Clink-clink-clink went the sound. He never wanted for soup, nor a place to rest his head (the occasional park bench notwithstanding), and though he played his hayseed's heart out six days a week, paying tribute to the hymns of the south, not a single club owner downtown invited him to demonstrate his talent for a more respectable audience; that is, for people who paid to get in. Too prosaic for modern tastes, came the familiar refrain.

If ambition is to spring what failure is to winter, then Mort's hopes for success had entered the late stages of autumn. He knew the crowds would eventually tire of the freckled, bespectacled kid with lightning in his hands, and who stomped along while singing "Blessed Fountain of Blood," and "Bright Anticipation."

As expected, his cup did not runneth over. Longer intervals of silence came between the clinks, until one day he received only five tips, one for each finger on his fretting hand. Familiar faces in the crowd soon passed by without a glance in his direction.

Dejected, and with winter closing in, he meandered through town thinking he'd use the last of his money to get good and snockered, when a sound caught his ear. A new sound, unlike any he'd ever heard, the chords of this strange music tugging at the strings of his beleaguered spirit. He followed it through the gnarled traffic, and toward a section of town most folks with skin pale as bleached wood pulp avoided.

And there, exploding from the doors of a darkened bar came a sound to wake the dead, and get them dancing. Music not made in reverence to some higher power, but to the power of life itself. They called it jazz, and if not for the shock of hearing it played for the first time, Mort might have cried.

"Pardon me, Mister, but who's that on piano?" he asked a dapper, ebony-skinned man carrying a box toward the bar's entrance.

"That's The Reverend," he said, glancing at Mort as though he'd seen a leprechaun.

"Who?"

"Earl Haynes, man. Get your ears right."

Mort stood there an hour getting his ears right, and so moved was he by the music that he handed everything he'd earned the previous week to another man at the door, requesting he pass it on as a donation to The Reverend. So went the routine: Mort busking for change in the white area of town, then making a nightly donation to Earl Haynes and his band in the evenings. Sometimes he'd stand outside strumming along, until one night they invited him inside.

Mort explained it thus in a magazine article:

"I think they took pity on me. What else would you call it? Here's this raggedy white kid coming to pay his respects, peeking through the door and what not. They knew I meant well. And maybe word got inside I could play, though at the time banjo was strictly a southern thing, you know, a Dixieland thing. After sizing me up, Mr. Haynes, The Revered himself, let me sit in a couple of tunes, and that's how it all got started."

Mort put his own band together—Mort Gallagher's Red-Hot Rascals—and soon after took his first fateful sip of the Old Dread No. 9. The hits followed, as did the broken marriages, legal battles, back-alley brawls, bad investments, and poisonous flings. Then, at the height of his popularity nine years later (though by then he looked like someone who'd been spat out the end of a grain thresher), he vanished without a word. *Pouf!*

Some believed Mort had joined a cult, others thought mobsters had fitted him with brick ankle bracelets and dropped him into Lake Michigan. Others scoured his lyrics for clues, claiming he'd left a trail of bread crumbs for his devoted fans to follow. In the absence of facts, even wilder theories took flight, though none soared so high as to touch upon the truth. I now know what happened to Mort Gallagher. I believe I know what happens to all those who make it past the nine-year mark of their addiction to The Dread.

. . .

Back to my friend. My dear, doomed friend. We'll call him Mr. O. Unlike Mort, he never achieved much with his paintings, though not for a lack of talent or the ability to produce a viewable collection. No, it had more to do with confidence, or lack thereof, and the inability to manage the simplest of tasks and responsibilities. Some people, I believe, are born too sensitive. The slightest change in the weather can alter their moods so profoundly, you'd think they'd contracted some horrible disease. One wrong word or deed can send them spiraling. These hopeless neurotics see signs and patterns where none exist, believing an invisible force—call it fate—is out to destroy them, and only by divine providence do they persevere.

So describes Mr. O, the king of tortured souls, the victim of whim and weather.

I'll spare you the sordid details of his full decline, and cut right to his final days; days in which I'd lost all hope for his recovery, and sought only to keep him company. What else could I do? The Dread owned him, body and soul. However, unlike the hollowing effects of cocaine, absinthe, heroin, and hooch, the Dread keeps most artists working until the end, like a malevolent muse, cracking a whip.

This is how I found Mr. O. one rainy night in October, 1948.

Looking at the clock after dinner, I told my wife I needed to check in on him, and asked that she wrap some leftovers to go. The look she gave me contained a hundred past arguments about my foolish devotion to my friend, how he'd taken advantage of my kindness too many times, how he'd sworn over and over to get clean, only to disappoint me later; how his presence in our humble home caused her no little discomfort. But apart from tying him down and forcing him to ride out the withdrawal symptoms—potentially killing him in the process—I did the next best thing. I brought him dinner.

Meatloaf wrapped in foil in one hand, umbrella in the other, I bowed against the pelting rain and made the five-block trek to his below-ground studio flat on Pine Avenue, and tapped on the curbside window. The rain-smeared image within struck me as a portrait from Picasso's Blue Period. There sat the artist, sallow and slumped in front of his easel, staring into a white sheet covering the canvas, as though willing the image beneath to complete itself in secrecy. Empty bottles of Old Dread No. 9 littered every available space. Refuse and clothes lay strewn about the floor. A picture of sadness and isolation, of death.

I tapped again, louder.

Mr. O. roused from his lugubrious state, looked toward the window, and sneered. Recognizing me at last, his sneer turned to a half-formed smile, though resentment sill lingered in his grin. In that moment I regretted calling on him, and didn't I sense he held some resentment toward me? The road to Hell is paved with good intentions, or so the proverb goes.

In this case it's paved in wet cement, and it goes down. I passed beneath a waterfall of rain off a ledge as I descended the darkened stairwell. Before my knocking hand reached the door, the bolt turned, and no sooner opened did I catch the whiff of The Dread from inside: sickly-sweet, like an over-ripened plum stuffed in the mouth of a cadaver. I sealed my nostrils and breathed through my mouth, while trying to hide my shock at the sight of my friend's waxen complexion and disheveled appearance. Here stood a man in the final stages of dissolution. And though his features remained quite alluring, almost effeminate in nature, as they'd been in youth, the dark circles under his otherwise luminous eyes—a nocturne's eyes—suggested the temple of his body sought to evict its resident ghost.

"Brother," he said, offering me his handshake.

Receiving it, I withheld from squeezing too hard for fear of shattering his bones—cold bones, wrapped in a thin layer of skin just as easily torn.

"You're all wet," he said. Come in, come in."

He moved like an old man roused from a nap as I followed him inside. I tasted the Old Dread's deadly tonic on my tongue, and succumbed to breathing once again through my nose, thinking I'd better just get used to the stench. My God, he'd turned the place into a rat's nest. The flat contained a simple cot in the corner, a dank washroom no larger than a closet, and a kitchenette cluttered with coffee cans stuffed with old paint brushes. He'd stacked countless canvases against the walls, their images facing inward, hidden. Some he'd taken the trouble to hang, and the story they told, at least as I gleaned in a cursory glance, was one of endless searching: doorways within doorways, leading to other worlds, though not to places any sane person would choose to visit. Not sober, anyway.

And, of course, the bottles of Dread, everywhere.

His eyes glossed over at the sight of me. "So good to see you. Let me get you a chair." He looked around, as though he'd misplaced it.

"I can't stay long."

"No, no, no. Stay and talk, brother. I haven't seen you in so long." He found the chair hiding beneath a pile of clothes, disrobed it, and set it beside his stool near the hidden canvas. "No one ever comes around. I guess they don't like the smell of me, or the sight of me. Probably think I lost my damn mind. Well screw them!" he said, his ennui turning on a dime. "Friends don't do that. That's why were brothers. We were always brothers, weren't we?"

"Yes," I said, hoping to calm him.

Back to the sweetness: "You're a good man. You're so good you don't know how good you are. I idolize you. Always have.

Me? I'm all screwed up. I'm jig-sawed. Stuck in this goddamn squat. Listening to people walk by all day, talking to themselves." Now came tears of rage. "Yesterday this old bag lady kept screaming at the sky, like she was all smacked-up. Kept saying, 'Crows and cats do not get along, crows and cats do not get along!' Imagine listening to that for an hour. This place…"

"It sounds unpleasant."

"This isn't the arts district, it's a nut house." He wiped his runny nose with his sleeve, then dusted off the chair. "Come on, brother, sit a minute."

With some hesitation I sat. "Oh, I brought you this." I passed the foiled meatloaf, still warm in my hand, into his. He looked at it as though I'd handed him a puzzle.

"Thanks. I'll eat it later." He set it on a small table near the easel. I knew then it would sit there for days, hardening like a brick.

"You'd better eat your dinner, young man, before it gets cold."

"I will, I promise. It smells great. Monica made it?"

"Who else?"

"You got lucky with her. She's a good woman. I know she hates me, but she's a good woman, and I'm glad you found her."

I shifted in my chair. "So, what are we working on?"

It took him a moment to shift his attention toward the canvas. "This," he said, "this is something new. This is important."

Given the stained sheet covering it, I had to take his word.

"I feel like I'm breaking through. At forty I'm finally getting it. I'm getting it!"

He pulled the sheet aside, revealing his latest masterwork. I sat aghast. The twenty-four by thirty-six inch painting depicted a lighted entryway of sorts at the end of a rancid sewer. This doorway, if I might call it that, given its phosphorescent glow, had been painted onto brick at a cul-de-sac in the drainage system, below which a river of muck flowed through a metal grate. Vermin seemed to scurry along the walkways lining each side of the tunnel. The doorway itself resembled the filigreed border one might find on the cover of an old book, but inside all pretense to literary sophistication gave way to a hellish menagerie of gloomy, misshapen figures peeking back from the shadows, as if daring the viewer to enter. Some had sprouted horns, others wings. Some walked on insects' legs, while others lapped at rivulets of liquid flowing from pipes—purple-black, like the color of The Dread—their tongues the length of their tails. Many of the sewer's denizens were engaged in an orgy, limbs and tongues entangled, their genitalia rigid, ripe, and gaping. A dirty Dalinian scene. The brackish water flowing into the grate below the entryway drew the eye along with it, and back toward the painting's focal point. And then I saw it: the image of my friend holding court at the center of this phantasmagoric milieu, seated in the same chair I had only moments before placed thine own rump.

Portions of the painting remained incomplete, its paler brush strokes offering some relief to an otherwise convincing depiction of Hell. Completing a work such as this, I thought, might spell disaster for its creator; or, at the very least, madness. I pulled my eyes from the canvas, and found him staring into the world he'd created with desperation and longing.

"It's out there," he said.

I thought he'd meant "out there" to mean out of this world. But no. He meant it literally.

"It's out there and I'm going to find it. I just need to keep working. Another week, maybe two."

"What do you mean by 'find it'?"

His eyes welled wetter than the rain-slickened streets outside. "Heaven," he said. He reached out and touched the canvas, as one caresses the cheek of an adoring child.

"The world of heaven is within," I said. Anything to distract him from his delusion.

"No," he countered, his tears giving way to frustration. "It's somewhere here, in the city, and I'm going to find it." He reached for a bottle of The Dread, a small, squarish bottle, its glass dark as a witch's eyes. Finding it empty, he tossed it aside, then reached for another. He swigged deep, as though he'd been lost in a desert for days. While tipped back, I noticed the ribboned border on the bottle's label resembled the doorway to his world, to Heaven.

"Slow down. Take a breath."

His lips popped off the nozzle. "Why?"

"Because I don't want to walk in here one day and find you cold as a fish on that cot."

"You won't. I'll be there," he said, in reference to Elysium. He snapped out of it, then looked at me as though I'd just walked in. "I never asked how you've been. How are you, brother? I want to know. It's so great to see you."

Another shift in mood. I pivoted to keep up. "I've been... busy."

"Doing what?"

"My job."

"The advertising gig?"

I caught the subtle dig in his use of the word "gig," though I refrained from retaliating. "That, and a little writing on the side."

"You're too good to waste your ideas on toaster ovens and refrigerators."

"I need the money."

"Money? What's money?" he said. "I don't give a damn about money. It turns people into grubby little crumb-snatchers. Everyone cutting each other's throats just to get ahead. Makes me sick."

"When you have a family to take care of, it's fairly important."

I'd said the wrong thing. His mood darkened. Somewhere, far from the city we called home, both his children lived under a reliable roof, in the care of his ex-wife and a man who made a respectable living. A man he despised.

"I'm not so bad, am I? Tell me I'm not so terrible."

"You're troubled, and you're sick. There's a difference. You need to kick this poison once and for all."

"I know, and I will. I'll make you proud. And any money I make I'll give to my kids. I don't need much, anyway. Never did. I'd give them the world."

I hesitated telling him a letter of apology might be a good place to start. "Let me see you eat something before I go."

There sat the meatloaf in its foil, like a rock from some distant planet. He picked it up and opened it, then picked off little pieces and fed himself. After a few bites, he wiped his hands on his paint-smudged trousers, the catsup left behind blending in with the hues of Heaven.

"Eat the whole thing," I told him, rising. I took one last glance at the painting. "I might stop in tomorrow night."

"Please do, brother. Please do. I'll straighten up this dump, then we'll have a good time, just like the old days."

"Okay. You just keep your head on straight."

And with that, I left him to his dinner.

At work the following day, as I struggled to compose a snappy slogan and related copy about the latest wonder gadget Mills & Berg had been contracted to promote, I got to thinking about what Mr. O. had said about my personal writing: the poems and short stories I always tried to squeeze in before breakfast. And damn me if his comment didn't contain a thorn of truth. In fact, it stung. A reliable salary came with its own rewards, of course, but producing original work and finding a readership for it seemed a greater cause, though an unrealistic one, especially at the age of forty-one. I chewed my pencil, then stepped out to the building's tenth floor balcony for a cigarette. The rain showed no signs of letting up, and as I lit up, I let my gaze drift toward the squalid building in the arts district, where my friend, I assumed, had awoken sometime after one o'clock to begin his dabbing and brushing of Heaven's gate, all while feeding his addiction.

What subterranean horrors will he glimpse today? and did I really mean to visit him that evening? Could I bear another bout of his ever-shifting moods, and cavernous need for my approval? I found it all exhausting. Nothing I'd ever said swayed him toward cleaner living, and nothing short of a blood transfusion and thirty days in a good clinic would clear his mind.

And yet I loved him, despite his suicidal devotion to The Dread. Or maybe I loved the memory of the two of us as kids, running together through Dayspring Park, and sought only to recapture to that sunlit image in his presence. Looking back, three decades passed too fast, and led us on divergent paths. He'd remained true to his ambitions, though his dangerous impulses undermined his efforts, while I took the advice of my prefrontal cortex, and built a career. No two friends, I believe, had ever drifted farther apart while remaining in contact.

"Again? You were just there last night," Monica said, finishing her last bite of dinner. She always looked put together, even on a rainy Tuesday evening.

I set my napkin on the table and considered the subtext of her question and subsequent comment. In essence, she'd meant: Don't go down with the drowning man.

"He's got nobody else," I said at last.

"And whose fault is that?"

I conceded the point with a conciliatory tilt of my head.

She looked at my plate. "Are you finished?"

A smattering of peas lay among my well-picked chicken bones. "Yeah."

Monica took both plates into the kitchen and scraped the remains into the trash. The sound of her rinsing them off in the sink drowned out her next question.

"Say again?"

Seconds later she appeared in the entryway, looking weary. "I wish you wouldn't go."

Ah, not a question. The truth, spoken plainly. "I'm not really sure I want to."

"What did you tell him?"

"I told him *maybe* I'd stop by."

"Well, there you go. Reschedule," she said, stepping back into the kitchen.

"He's not the kind of person who keeps a schedule. He doesn't even wear a watch."

"Even better. Besides, I thought you had a lot of work to finish before tomorrow."

"I do," I said, dreading the mountain of work waiting for me in the den. The client wanted a complete campaign proposal by end of week, including a budget for print and radio ad buys. This of course involved a complex mechanism of writers, illustrators, typesetters, and voice personalities I'd later set loose on an unsuspecting public, convincing them to buy something they didn't need. In this case, a stand mixer boasting a quieter performance than its predecessor, thanks to its new motor and dual, stainless-steel whisks. My head hurt just thinking about it.

"I should just get it over with. Do we have any leftover chicken?"

"Sure do, Florence Nightingale."

"Ha, ha, ha," I said, deadpan.

"You won't be laughing when Frank calls you into the office tomorrow expecting to see some progress."

"Yeah, well, Frank isn't dying, is he?"

I'd said it without thinking, and knew it to be true. Mr. O. had a date with the gate, which I realized, sitting in my dull, but well-ordered dining room, represented a passageway between this life and the next; between banality and splendor, no matter how dark its conceptualization.

More rain. Heavier. Colder.

Sloshing through the downtown streets beneath my umbrella I turned with a start at the sound of men laughing. A couple of derelicts in the alley to my left had managed to get a fire going in a trash can, the steel awning above it catching dark plumes of ember-speckled smoke.

"Mr. Businessman," one of the bundled men said through a matted beard, "where you going? You don't belong down here. Nobody needs your insurance policy or your legal advice."

"I do," his thinner cohort said. "I got a woman who stole all my money, and I want it back. Help me out, Mr. Businessman. I'll make you rich."

Both men laughed.

I picked up my pace and hung a left at Third Avenue—a brighter street than the one I'd chosen in order to save time—and soon arrived at the narrow, street-level window of one Mr. O.

"What the hell happened here?"

Mr. O. sat slouched in the corner of his studio, staring through his tousled bangs at the washroom's toilet; a thing he'd beaten to death with a hammer. Water had seeped into the main living area, pushing aside the dust bunnies and dirt in its path. He'd left the murder weapon hanging from a hole in the wall.

"There's something in there," he said, clutching tight to a bottle of Dread, his dirty thumbnail scratching away at the label. The meatloaf I'd brought the previous evening lay hardening on the table near the easel.

"Probably the thing you put in it."

"I didn't crap in there, if that's what you're saying."

"Then what?"

"Something like an octopus. I don't know. It touched me. I jumped up, then I saw it just... slither back down." A mournful beat followed. "Is it still there?"

I stepped around the puddle and leaned into the water closet to look. I pulled a string connected to a bare lightbulb, and by its harsh light I saw nothing amidst the shards of porcelain to suggest some aquatic lifeform had come to tickle his nether regions.

"Nothing."

"You sure?"

"Sure, I'm sure. Do you have a mop?"

"I swear I saw it."

"And I believe you. Do you have a mop?"

He took a long draught of No. 9. "No. But maybe some towels under the sink?"

"And put that down, would you? You've clearly gone past your limit."

"There are no limits."

"When you get the idea to smash your own toilet, I'd say there are limits!"

I rather liked the heat my anger unleashed in my body, considering I'd shivered the entire way to his squalid studio, which lacked heating, or much else resembling modern amenities; certainly not the Weber & Co. Model X7 Stand Mixer with dual, stainless-steel whisks.

Quiet as a hummingbird.

Not bad, I thought, wondering if I could convince Weber & Co. to use the image of the hummingbird as part of their logo. At the very least, I had something to pitch Frank, my ever-frazzled boss, tomorrow morning. I came across a few stiff towels under the sink, and got to work sopping up the spill.

"Just leave it. I'll take care of it," he said.

"Okay." I stood and held out a towel, keeping it well out of reach.

He braced his back against the wall and inched upward on his clavicles, until he more or less stood upright. Two steps in my direction and he wilted, his eyes losing focus. I dropped the towel and grabbed hold of him before he had the chance to fall and split open his head.

"Good catch," he said, as I guided his frail, teetering frame onto the cot. "Hey, remember that time we climbed that huge tree at the park?"

I feigned ignorance while lifting his legs onto the dingy mattress.

"Remember?"

I couldn't hold back a frustrated sigh. "Yes, I remember."

"I'd climbed higher than you. So high. I remember looking down at you. Oh man, the look on your face," he said, his grin revealing a row of rotted, Dread-stained teeth. "You were so scared. But then I kept going… up, up, up. The branches got thinner, thinner, and then…"

"And then you slipped."

"But you caught me, brother. You caught me!" He grabbed my arm, as if to remind me of my own grip. "My legs were swinging midair. I thought we'd both die."

"We almost did."

He released my arm. "You're still catching me, aren't you?"

I took the bottle from his hand and set it on the floor. "Get some rest. Tomorrow, I'm taking you to see a doctor," I said, easing him into a prostrate position and positioning a pillow beneath his head. Rain-streaked light through the window seemed to melt his features.

"I don't need a doctor. I need to finish my painting." His eyes slid toward his masterpiece, and across his murky orbs I swear I caught the gleam of figures moving and writhing in reflection. I turned to confirm what my eyes mistook for motion. Sure enough, none of the figures on the canvas so much as twitched; however, the doorway to his world seemed brighter than the night before, though I attributed this increased luminescence to an additional layer of pigment he'd applied before my arrival.

"You're going to the doctor tomorrow, and then you're going to get well, and then I won't have to you catch you anymore. You'll be able to catch yourself."

"Sure, pal," he said with a beatific grin. "Sure." His cold hand patted mine.

"I'm serious."

"I'm serious, too." His heavy eyelids told a different story: one of endless sleep. He whispered: "You look like one of them."

"Who?" I asked, not wanting to know the answer.

His eyes drifted toward the canvas behind me.

"Just get some sleep."

Then, in barely a breath: "Okay, pal, okay."

You'll never know the relief I felt when his eyelids closed without reopening. I sat on the edge of the cot for a few minutes listening to the rain, as I watched his chest rise and fall, rise and fall, thinking peace lay somewhere between each gentle breath, for all of us. I'll confess to you now, in those moments of non-breathing; in that strange, dark valley where nary a wheeze dared blow, I pictured him lying still as stone in a casket designed to look like a bottle of The Dread, his sad epitaph written in cursive on the lid's label:

Here lies Mr. O. Tortured painter, absent father, hoarder of sweeter seasons, and friend to one gullible bastard who tried to save him.

With my friend lost in a world of dreams I preferred *not* to imagine, I decided to straighten up his studio, so that he'd at least wake in a space less cluttered and stifling than the one between his ears. I began with the water on the floor—Lake Dread, I'd dubbed it—then collected the garbage and threw it away. I tossed the meatloaf and replaced it with the chicken I'd brought. Thinking twice, I threw that away, too. Next came the collecting of bottles. I found forty-eight bottles hiding in plain sight, like rotted easter eggs placed there by the Devil.

Clink-clink-clink went the sound as I gathered them together on the sink's the counter, now clean enough to prepare food on, excluding the moldy loaf of bread I found in the cupboard. In my continued rummaging, I opened a drawer and found a collection of men's wallets inside, each empty. I knew then how Mr. O. funded his habit, those delicate painter's hands of his equal to the task of pilfering pockets. For all my friend's noble talk about the corrupting influence of money, it seemed he needed it just like every other dollar-chasing sod in the city. Moreso, perhaps.

Discovering this secret, I believe most self-respecting people would have walked, but I, the Florence Nightingale of Pine Avenue, the legal representative and insurance agent to downtrodden fire-stokers everywhere, decided to stay. I've had plenty of time to reflect upon my decision, and have since concluded that my inclination to help Mr. O. bore little resemblance to altruism or loyalty. I got something out of it, didn't I?

I got to relish in the twin virtues of heroism and martyrdom, each feeding the other. And didn't the contrast between his dismal existence and mine not lend credibility to the choices I'd made? Furthermore, why did I require such a tawdry example of life gone awry to bolster my own sense of equilibrium?

Well, I'll tell you, though it pains me to admit it. It had to do with artistic pursuit. He'd chased his visions most of his adult life, sacrificing financial advancement, relationships, and even his health for time. I, on the other hand, had kept my visions—that paltry stack of stories and pseudo-poems I'd written before breakfast—in a drawer at home, where no one could find them. I suppose I wanted to see if he could lift himself out of the muck, and soar. After all, if he could do it, then so could I.

Pathetic, I know.

None of these insights came to my aid that evening, of course, and as I perused the paintings he'd leaned face-first against the wall, I noticed a gradual gradation—or degradation—toward darker themes and colors toward the back of the stack, with the final few (and most recent, I deduced) bearing a close resemblance to the unfinished painting on the easel.

What did I find in those previous, discarded experiments? Moth-faced men cavorting with spider-eyed women. Insects with billowing fins nibbling at pustules on another man's face; a face not so different in contour than my own. Even the brown fedora the character wore at a clever tilt resembled the one I donned each day. I wrote it off as coincidence at best, and an unconscious desire on Mr. O.'s part to see me diseased and suffering at worst.

Who knew what lurked in the basement of his imagination? Either way, I'd seen enough, and as I grabbed my coat, hat, and umbrella, I noticed I'd left a bottle of The Dread resting beside Mr. O.'s cot.

Let's get this out of the way now. In fact, let's say it together:

"Don't do it, you idiot!"

Excellent. Well done.

I stood there a moment thinking I should pour that noxious substance down the drain, but feared the consequences of depriving my friend's blood stream of its required nutrients. Going cold turkey from one day to the next could kill him. Taking care not to disturb him, I picked it up and inspected the label, some portions of which he'd scratched off with his thumbnail. To my shock and chagrin, I noticed a tiny, two-dimensional hummingbird captured mid-flight between a break in the label's ribboned border—toward the bottom, I might add, where few would notice. At first glance it appeared to drink from a bouquet of flowers. Not so. It's long, graceful beak pointed toward a trio of skulls blooming from a leafy stem.

Had I seen the hummingbird before and not noticed?

This is how it begins.

This is how The Dread draws you in.

I unscrewed the cap and took a whiff. My head spun, and while rotating, the images and characters from some of my stories appeared as if spinning on a carousel, their faces blurred at first, then sharpening in focus. Hurry up, they seemed to say. Publish your work. The world needs to know us, and we it.

All that from a single sniff. My curiosity, along with the desire to see more, got the better of me. What's the worst that could happen? I thought. After all, I'd been borne of tougher stuff than my friend. I knew how to organize my day and follow through on my commitments. I wore a tweed, three-piece suit and carried an expensive watch in my pocket, which always ticked close to my heart, reminding me to mind the hours. I'd saved enough money to send my son to college. Not the best college, but a college all the same. And so, adorned with my accomplishments while having no fear of falling prey to my baser instincts, I took a generous swig of Old Dread No. 9.

Gulp.

Liquid moonlight caressed my throat and soothed my spirit as it travelled down to the lower coils. It then shot back up in concentric waves of energy, like a Jacob's ladder. Within seconds it began breaking down my familiar associations with the objects in the studio. For example, the broken toilet in the washroom suddenly fascinated me to no end, not only from a visual perspective (a porcelain portal molded to fit our backsides), but in its choice of material, construction, and intended purpose. It whisks away the foulness in our bodies—out to the ocean, out of sight. It prevents disease and makes life bearable. It allows us to squat in private, and preserve some semblance of human dignity. Two restrooms in a household saves marriages. Three thrones, and you're a king. And what about all those pipes laid underground? Think of the sewers! Miles upon miles of brick-lined tunnels running beneath the living city, like bowels.

Just like the sewer tunnel in Mr. O's painting.

I turned toward the canvas. Oh, I'd been a fool to doubt my friend's attempt to portray the fluidity of matter and spirit in his work. The characters' transmutations toward the monstrous seemed a cause for celebration, not sorrow. Their shared levity bore them up, well above the river of muck flowing beneath their feet; the same muck from which our species had first arisen, shaking off the slime over time, then turning its collective gaze toward the stars.

In a cosmic blink, those same creatures learned to tell themselves stories, all of which posed the same two questions: Why am I here? and which way the restroom?

One swig of The Dread, and the magnificent complexity of

life lay at my fingertips.

Imagine living off the stuff for years, with no hope or desire of ever placing your feet back on the ground. I studied the bottle's label with renewed interest. Ah, the hummingbird, sipping nectar from a skull; the entirety of human existence captured in a single image.

~

Few folks on earth smoke with the same fanatical frequency as people who work in the advertising business. Journalists, maybe. Gumshoe detectives and men who bet their hard-earned dollars at the track, sure. But ad men take to nicotine like hummingbirds do skulls.

I'm no exception. I lit up and added to the thickening cloud of smoke in the tenth-floor conference room of Mills & Berg, thinking I'd soon blow the garters off my colleagues' socks with my astounding promotional pitch for the Weber X7 Stand Mixer with dual, stainless-steel whisks—a marvel of modern engineering sure to bring joy to domestic chefs everywhere. Put in the flour, put in the eggs, put in the butter and cream, and watch the whisks go round and round, all with improved performance and a quieter sound. From flaky pie crusts to fluffy biscuits, it does it all. And clean-up's a piece of cake.

Piece of cake, I wrote on my notepad. Or better yet: *Get cooking!*

As for The Dread, its effects had mellowed around bedtime, and no sooner than I closed my eyes did my cherished visions returne. You see, I used to play this game as a youngster, in which I'd lie in bed at night and mentally manipulate forms, shapes, and patterns, sometimes twisting the raw material of my imagination into architectural masterpieces. I had done this without effort for years, until one night it stopped, I believe around the time my career got going. But last night when I closed my eyes the visions exploded in three-dimensional glory, having been trapped so long in my skull like a jack-in-the-box, waiting to spring forth. And my dreams... such strange, wonderful dreams. They carried me to places I yearned to revisit upon waking. I give full credit to Old Dread No. 9, of course—to Inamorata, Lollygag, the libation with many names. I'm embarrassed to admit I longed for another swig; something to get me through the meeting, through the day, through this life.

And just look at all the sour pusses around me at the table. My colleagues looked like pallbearers at their own funerals, as they fiddled with their pens and pads of paper, adjusted their ties, as if to strangle themselves, and smoked themselves into oblivion. Not a single smile to go around. Gladys Montgomery, the department secretary, and the only woman in a room of eight men, seemed especially perturbed this morning. Someone brought up the subject of golf. Another complained about the rain.

I turned my attention to the Model X7 positioned in the center of the conference table, its gleaming, aeronautic design lending it the look of a commercial airliner. On the walls around me hung posters of other products we'd promoted in the past, ranging from automobiles to exercise equipment. Not quite the gallery in which someone might hang a convincing replica of the Mona Lisa, but good enough by Mills & Berg's standards. And I'd played an important role in the company's success.

What did Mr. O. have to show in comparison to this? Mr. O.! I'd forgotten about my promise to take him to see a doctor.

The heavy oak doors swung open, and in came Frank Mills, my boss, and to my horror—indeed to the horror of everyone in the room—Mr. Weber himself followed. A man with a lobster's complexion, and who spoke as if through a bullhorn, pronouncing to anyone within two blocks that they were in the presence of greatness. He smacked Frank on the shoulder and chuckled, as if he'd just told him a dirty joke.

Behind Mr. Weber came a weasel of a yes-man in round spectacles, known to all in the room as Mr. Weber's number two—one part attorney, ten parts pain in the backside. He drew as much air from a room as Mr. Weber added to it.

I stood up and plastered on a smile. Everyone else followed suit, including Jerry Porter, an ambitious young man who'd been gunning for my job for over a year.

"Well, good morning, everybody!" Mr. Webster announced.

Good mornings all around.

"And what a glorious day it is. Rain's good for the soul, I say. Good for the soul."

"Indeed," Frank said, motioning for Mr. Weber to take a seat at the head of the table. We all sat once Mr. Weber settled. His yes-man sat beside him with an inscrutable expression. All business. All numbers. All legalities.

Mr. Weber's eyes alighted upon the mixer. "Ah, and there she is. Ain't she a beaut?"

"She most certainly is," Jerry, the suck-up, said. "I was just commenting to my wife—"

"Got a hundred-thousand units coming hot off the line in Nebraska," Mr. Weber said, cutting him off, "with another three hundred thousand on the way. Time is of the essence, gentleman. The absolute essence. The holidays are upon us, and I want one of these damn things in every kitchen across America before Thanksgiving, so let's get cooking! What do we got?"

Damn, he stole my line! My stomach tightened.

Frank cleared his throat. "As you know, we've had our star-hitter, Tom Maxwell, on the job. You may remember Tom from the Kitchen Master Plus campaign."

I nodded to Mr. Weber.

"How could I forget?" he said. "Did so well I bought the

missus a vacation home in Florida. Cozy little place right on the beach, until a monsoon came along and blew the roof off the son of a bitch." He chortled. "Oh, well. Lay it on me, Mr. Maxwell."

"Mr. Weber," I began, "how quiet would you say the Model X7 is?"

"Quiet. The quietest model yet."

"If you had to compare it to something, I mean."

"I don't know, it's quiet."

"Quiet as a..." I waited for him to fill in the blank, but he just stared at me. I stood and clicked on the machine, setting it to the highest speed. The spinning blades produced a hum similar to that of a hummingbird's wings. I turned it off, and said, "Consider the hummingbird, Mr. Weber—fast, graceful, colorful; a symbol of spring, of sweetness. I would venture to say the Model X7 is—" I let the moment build "—quiet as a hummingbird."

You could hear a mouse pass gas in the silence that followed. Jerry, the kid who'd been waiting for my slightest misstep, pursed his lips to stifle a grin.

"What's this about hummingbirds?" Mr. Weber wanted to know, turning to Frank.

Frank jumped in to save me. "I'm sure Tom's got more up his sleeve." Frank shot me a look that suggested: *abort, abort!*

But I'd been touched by The Dread, and had no intention of aborting. I had a vision, damnit, and I just needed to prove to Mr. Weber that this product required a fitting symbol to offset its hefty construction. "Did you know the North American hummingbird beats its wings fifty times per second, the same approximate rate as that of the X7's whisks? No mere coincidence. In fact, I'd call it serendipity. And the image of the bird itself..."

Frank looked to be on the verge of a coronary, but I pressed on.

"...does it not appeal to the sensibilities of the gentler sex? Imagine that image emblazoned across the front panel, here," I said, gesturing like a sommelier displaying a fine bottle of wine.

"Why is he going on about hummingbirds?" Mr. Weber asked Frank. Then, turning to me, "Stop, stop, stop. Sure, the X7 is quiet, but that's not the main... uh, what do you call it?" he said, turning to the weasel.

"Selling point."

Mr. Weber smacked the table. "That's it: selling point."

"And if I'm not mistaken," the weasel continued, "Hoyt uses a hummingbird image on their sewing machines. We'll look into it, of course."

"No. No one needs to look into it. Here's how we sell this son of a bitch. It's powerful and built to last. We smacked a lifetime guarantee on this thing. *And... and* it's quiet. Why? The angle of the blades on its whisks. My boys spent moths dialing that in. Let's talk about that. Better yet, what do you think, young lady? Why should every woman in America want to own one of these units?"

He'd posed the question to Gladys, and with Mr. Weber's attention on her, Frank motioned for me to sit down and zip it up. I did, my cheeks burning and my ego bruised.

"Well," Gladys said, "I guess it would make their jobs in the kitchen a little easier. I wouldn't know, as I can't even burn toast the right way."

"You don't cook?" Mr. Weber said, dumfounded.

"No, sir. Not really. My husband does the cooking."

Another shock. "And does he wear an apron?"

Gladys gave the question serious consideration. "Sometimes."

Jerry Porter took the floor before Mr. Weber's face turned redder. "I propose we sell it with the end-product in mind," he said. "Sure, it's a beautiful unit. It's quiet, but think of what you can create with it: pies, cakes, pastries... we fill the adds up with these images, so that you can almost smell them through the print. Or how about this? Television! Rather than talking about how great the product is, we show the audience by way of demonstration. Hire some wholesome yet attractive Betty or Helen to run it through its paces. And get this: on set, we include all the other great products Weber has to offer. She mixes the dough with X7, she puts a Weber tray into a... that's right, a Weber oven; she uses a Weber blender; she uses Weber utensils. See where I'm going with this?"

Mr. Weber's eyes widened as he imagined the possibilities, and just like that the account slipped from my fingers.

There are low points and there are low points. Some involve soup. And as I sat staring into a bowl of chicken soup placed on the table by Monica, I got the itch to get the heck out of the house.

"What's the matter?"

I looked around the room. Everything in perfect order. Everything dusted. It even smelled pleasant. *She* smelled pleasant, like a prairie after a rain.

"You ever get bored with all of this?"

"What do you mean?"

"I don't know. Bored with routine. Bored with taking care of the house and preparing meals. Bored with... just bored. Bored, bored, bored."

"Are we talking about you or me?"

"I'm asking if you're bored."

"Well, it's no secret I've wanted to travel when the weather improves and we've saved up a little money."

I crumbled some crackers and dropped them in the soup. Even they looked bored, floating there among bits of chicken and carrots. "I'm going out."

"Where?"

"I promised ____ I'd take him to get some help."

"At this hour?"

"It's only eight o'clock," I reminded her, stepping into the foyer and snatching my hat, trench coat, and umbrella.

"At least take a cab," she said. "I don't like the look of those people who slum around his apartment."

"They're all right," I told her. "Besides, I'm their official insurance agent and legal representative."

"What on earth are you talking about?"

"Nothing. It's a joke."

Mr. O. didn't answer the door, so I ran back up the stairwell and peered through the window as the rain beat a tattoo on my umbrella. Vacant.

I wandered deeper into the downtown district to look for him, the streets aglow from lighted signs above, each advertising mundane services—shoe repair, sewing machine repair, tax preparation services. I could see why he worked so hard to reconfigure the matter of ordinary things in his paintings. Who wanted to wander through a world grown dull, living only to fulfill a never-ending series of perfunctory tasks? When I looked at a street sign or a building, I wanted to see something more than lighted temples dedicated to the gods of consumerism. And when I stared into something as common as a toilet, I wanted to know where the dirt went after the flush. Down, into the sewers, I thought. The sewers, where rats scurry about their ratty business, where things stir in the muck, and where doorways open, leading to new worlds; a place in which a troubled artist hooked on Old Dread No. 9 might find solace, even if only in his imagination.

. . .

My wanderings led me deeper into a maze of buildings and narrow, one-way streets, their uneven sidewalks littered with trash, and where trees lacking in ambition sprouted from protective, metal picket barriers. I peered down darkened alleyways as I strode along, marveling at the twin waterfalls drizzling from rooftops between them, then paused to light a cigarette. While propping my umbrella in the crook of my arm and striking a match, a man rounded the corner ahead of me at a panicked clip, as though fleeing something terrible he'd either witnessed or done. I had little time to react.

He raised his elbows and plowed through me, knocking the air from my lungs, the umbrella from my hand, and my body to the cold, wet cement. The back of my head thudded hard on the pavement. The stars in my vision intermingled with the sheets of rain darting past the lights spilling through the upper-story windows. I rolled over, soaked and cursing, and saw my assailant disappear into the shadows, coattails flapping, the sound of his steps receding, receding.

Hit and run. Bastard.

Once my head cleared, I stood and performed a systems check. Everything seemed in proper working order, though my head throbbed like the dickens. Not so bad, I should say, as to dissuade me from investigating whatever had transpired in the alley. I retrieved the umbrella. Raising it over my head seemed moot at this point, given my sodden state, so instead I collapsed it, thinking its point might make a decent stabbing weapon should I encounter trouble.

And so, armed with my umbrella, I entered the alley.

The shadows there seemed darker, the rain rainier, if such a thing were possible, and as I ventured deeper in the chasm, I got to thinking about the bowl of soup I'd left cooling on the dining room table at home. Shouldn't I turn around right here and now? I wondered. Shouldn't I get a good night's rest, then wake nice and early tomorrow morning and figure out a way to wrest the Weber account from the hands of my young adversary, Jerry Porter?

A man consumed by practicalities and the desire to advance his career might think so. Not I, the secretive scribbler of stories and poems. Not I, the urban argonaut, who sought fresh meaning and surprises where others saw signs and buildings. I wanted to see more. And my God, did I see it!

I raised my flimsy weapon as I trod through deeper puddles in the alley, my soaked socks freezing my feet. But I didn't care, fixated as I was on something disturbing the shadows some twenty yards ahead. Just then a man cried out in agony, his voice echoing in a canyon of concrete. With a thousand needles of fear pricking my skin, I advanced, the silver point of my black umbrella leading the way. When I drew closer to these garbled sounds of anguish, I caught sight of a pair of legs writhing slowly behind the dumpster, their owner hidden from view.

My first thought: Here lies a victim of the same man who'd rammed me earlier—stabbed, then left to bleed out in the alley, though I saw no blood intermingling in the puddle in which I walked, only a thin layer of motor oil glistening like a filthy rainbow on its surface. All things considered, including my own safety, I crept around the dumpster and parried at a male figure squirming in a pile of refuse, his sudden and violent paroxysms accompanied by the sound of chicken bones being ripped from their sockets: deep and wet, the cartilage cracking. Another sound I first mistook as rotted leftovers smooshing beneath the man's body proved to be something far worse. It was the sound of his flesh and innards slithering and gurgling together, like a big sack of slugs with salt thrown on them. It seemed he'd soon burst from the casing of his skin.

Following this traumatic discovery came two horrifying realizations—the first, that the man twitching and whimpering in the garbage was none other than Mr. O, his facial features twisting themselves in the shape of his pain, and second, that his body sought to unmake itself; or rather, *remake* itself in the image of his painted nightmares. In blind desperation he reached toward me, but no sooner his wrist snapped backward, the fingers contorting at each joint and pointing in confused directions.

He shouted from the depth of his diaphragm. If people in the apartments above heard, none opened their windows to tell him to shut up. I however nearly fainted while witnessing this transformation, for what else could it be? When a wave of nausea and encroaching darkness passed, I willed myself to take hold of his hand. His fingers wrapped around my wrist, though backwards, his joints snapping into place like a clamp. The sensation sent a shockwave of primordial fear through my body, and in my effort to pull away I lifted him to his feet, and into a faint shaft of sallow light.

Here, all rationality fled, as before me stood not my friend, but something dredged from a bog or a sewer—an amphibious insect, his parts all askew—*jig-sawed,* as he'd stated only two days prior in his studio. The flesh of his face roiled, then his jaw snapped open and slackened down to his chest. Out came a grayish tongue long-enough to slither between the thighs of five lovers: the perfect instrument of pleasure. And let me not forget his eyes, for this aspect of his continued reconfiguration struck me as the most terrifying. Once pale blue, they now swirled with a liquid not unlike the color of The Dread—purple-black, yes, but containing glints of phosphorescence that overtook his irises. Worse, the look behind the eyes spoke not of sorrow, but a pained kind of joy. Then, as if to ward me away forever, his eyes protruded from their sockets like twin, gelatinous eels, the capillaries within growing redder thicker toward the roots. The elongated eyes bent midair, and slithered closer to mine. I tried to pull away, but his grip tightened as he pulled me close. He wanted me to see the true being behind the mask, it seemed, to know he'd found salvation at last.

Point well-received, his eyes retracted, and he released me. I fell backwards with a jarring splash. While sitting like a stick in the mud, I watched his body run through its final stages of transfiguration, his sockets and joints re-fastening themselves to his reformed anatomy, the bones therein clicking into place, leaving his elbows and knees inverted. His drenched hair slithered free from his scalp, and his skin acquired the biofluorescent hue of a salamander. He retracted his tongue and raised a finger, as if to say "watch." Then, to my utter repulsion—though I found it difficult to look away—he stripped off his clothes, starting with the threadbare blazer he wore seven days a week. He whipped it high in the air, then threw it aside. Next came the shirt, then the slacks. I should say here there are certain things about our friends we might be curious about, but don't really want to see, but with his transformation came a kind of hedonistic freedom on his part, along with a madhouse grin as he lowered his shorts and unveiled... *It.* No other word for it. Suffice it to say he'd never lack in romantic interest, neither from women nor men, nor any being between.

This final bit of clothing tossed aside, he looked up and said in a gurgling voice: "Brother. I know where to go. Do you want to see?"

"See what?" I said, quivering from head to toe.

"Heaven, pal. Heaven. Keep up, if you can."

And with that he dashed stark nude toward a tall, chain-link fence at the end of the alley.

There are visions and there are visions. Some take place in sewers.

I tried my best to follow, but I hadn't run at full speed or climbed a fence since my teenage years, and at forty-one (with thirty additional pounds at my waist), I struggled to climb. He waited for me at the top, straddling the bar, and said, "Come on, slow-poke," just like when we were kids, and damn me if the ploy didn't work. I climbed faster, not giving a second thought to the rusted wires threatening to cut open my fingers.

He chuckled, then jumped. No sooner than his feet hit the ground did he sprint at an inhuman pace toward a narrow street running perpendicular to the alley, where he made a hard right. I clambered up and over, determined to keep pace, even if my nicotine-stained lungs and pounding heart cautioned otherwise. Men my age and in similar physical condition died of lesser thrills and exertions. But talk of seeing Heaven firsthand (witnessing his transformation, I believed every word) lent speed to my underworked limbs. I knew I'd pay the price the following day, but knowing did not mean slowing. I turned right, and slid in a pool of grease oozing from a row of trash cans behind a restaurant. Down I went, palms slapping hard on concrete. I looked up. The naked loon continued deeper down the street, whooping and hollering, calling out to the world to behold the glorious actualization of art-in-man. All he lacked was a big bright moon.

My jealousy knew no bounds.

Up again, running, stray cats leaping out of my path, I held him within my sights at a hundred-yard distance. The rain showed no signs of abating, and through the downpour I missed his next turn, for the street ahead lay empty, apart from a few parked vehicles. Left of right, I didn't know, until I heard a distant cry of freedom. The Dread-borne banshee had headed toward the downtown district's industrial sector. I gave chase, though my fall and previous sprint left me limping. A sharp pain in my side threatened to stop me in my tracks, and my lungs felt like two furnace chambers pumping heat into Hades. I had no choice but to trod along while gathering my breath. If not for his continued cries of liberation, for his delirious cackling and sudden bursts into song, I might have lost him in the maze completely.

I ran past a series of manufacturing facilities, their wrought iron gates and fences topped with barbed wire, warding off trespassers and thieves, though I doubted they'd prevent my friend from scaling them. I reached a scrapyard at the end of the street and looked in both directions. I'd lost him; rather, he'd lost me. Bent over and heaving for breath, I began to lose hope of seeing Mr. O.'s final departure from the solid state of reality. Then I heard it: a grinding metallic sound, followed by a deep clank in the next alley over. A sewer lid, I assumed, lifted and slid from its hole, then dropped. And did his triumphant voice not echo in the depths of a tunnel?

Consider the hummingbird. Consider the sewer. Consider the malleable properties of flesh and bone, and what the dreaming mind can achieve.

I jogged in pursuit of his straight-jacketed serenade, which grew fainter by the second, then came upon an open entryway leading to the city's bowels. It seemed he'd tossed the sewer lid aside with ease, as it lay ten feet from the hole. I stood over the black pit, the rain running past my feet and down into it, and feared, in my all-too-human condition, the foulness I'd encounter once I descended. The sound of rats in the sewer affirmed my fears.

Down I went, clinging tight to the rungs of a steel ladder, and thinking myself a fool as inky shadows enveloped me. Somewhere below a river, which smelled like rotted mushrooms and sulfur, rushed along the tunnel as it made its way toward the ocean. I descended deeper, but my foot failed to make contact with another rung. Not knowing how much distance lay between my dangling foot and the ground (or maybe the river itself), I negotiated the remaining rungs with my arms alone, feet groping for purchase like antennae; then, stretched to the full length of my body, I made contact with cement and released the ladder. Looking up at the faint circle of light through which I'd passed, I gauged my altitude at thirty feet below street level. No sooner estimated, something scurried across my right foot. I kicked instinctively, and sent a rat squeaking down the river, its friends along the narrow walkway on which I stood cheering it on.

By the sound of it, Mr. O. had taken a right turn down the tunnel, in the direction of the rushing sewage. Thinking I'd slip and drown in the population's collective stew of processed mutton and potatoes, of beer, bread, and swine, I reached into my coat's inner pocket and retrieved my book of matches. They felt damp in my hand, but perhaps dry enough to strike. After three fumbling tries, fire flared from my fingers, and I gained some sense of the brick-lined Hell I'd entered, the end of which terminated in darkness, with the rancid river flowing into it. Then I saw the rats, everywhere: wet-furred, bald-tailed, whiskered, and far too bold for my liking. They regarded me with little ruby eyes, then scattered in profusion at the sound of my voice and stamping of my foot.

"Go! Get out of here! Get!"

The match went out. I struck another. The rats kept their distance, like curious onlookers waiting for an accident to happen. And wouldn't I provide a fine feast if I drowned? As it stood, the narrow walkway allowed for little error, but sensing I'd soon lose my friend altogether, I pressed on in a flickering pool of light, holding onto the match as long as I could. Each time one went out my heart quickened, and with only five or six left at my disposal, the certainty of returning back the way I came in total darkness caused me no little panic.

The price of Heaven: fear.

I soon caught up to the sound of Mr. O.'s singing, his wavering, aquatic tones motivating me to move faster. I reached another turning point. Right, I decided, after discerning the direction of his voice. To my relative relief the tunnel here widened, and seemed free of rats. And the water, having entered a wider canal, moved a little slower, though still fast enough to drown an advertising man in a drenched, three-piece suit.

I came upon a gentle downward slope leading to a wider area, though the low ceiling before me obscured the true height and width of the chamber beyond. Then the match went out. Cursing, I lit another. Only three matches remained. With extreme gratitude, I gripped a handrail running alongside a descending cement stairway, the rain water and muck cascading alongside it. Down it went into a veritable black lake inside a massive cistern, its brick pillars and archways lending it the look of an underground cathedral, a place where gilled maidens and dead mariners found romance, though this illusion fell away at the sight of a turbine. The metal structure hummed and churned, drawing in water, and feeding the city with electricity.

I quickly learned I wasn't alone, for at the far end of the cistern a phosphorescent glow cast an entranceway of sorts across the roiling water, its shape similar to the ribboned doorway in Mr. O.'s painting, and to the border on a bottle of The Dread. The cistern's overlapping archways hid the source of light, but not the sound emanating from it. Music. And not just any music, but music for the mad, for the love-drunk; for poets and painters who drank words and pigment, and passed vowels and rainbows. Strings and harps and woodwinds seemed to chase one another around and around along a melodic theme so lilting, so filled with yearning, that I thought my soul might burst from my body at hearing it. It seemed to represent music in its absolute purest form, like the stuff of dreams, ever-flowing and surprising, yet making a strange kind of sense, and did the notes not dance in filaments of lavish light?

The match went out, but the light at the far end of the

cistern grew brighter, and by its bluish haze and golden tendrils of sound, which slithered along the ceiling, licking the bricks, I ventured down into the cathedral, and toward the entrance to Heaven.

I dropped to my knees at the shimmering sight across the water. Tears flowed from my eyes. If the final aim of art was to cast light into the darkness, to illuminate the unknown and lead people of the solid, rational world in a dream-state toward Nirvana, toward their true and final home, then the vision before me exceeded this aesthetic aspiration in spades. Mr. O.'s depiction came close in approximating the vision before me, except in the execution of color. Had I never opened my eyes until this moment? Had I not truly considered the hummingbird?

Had I never known, except for a few ragged remnants of dreams recalled upon waking, what beautiful creatures we could all become, if we only imagined it? The world beyond Mr. O.'s portal teamed with fantastical life, and they lived in such luxury, such dignity, that the richest of Rockefellers would drain their fortunes to own it. And yet, it sprung from the mind of the poorest person I knew. I smelled lavender and the smoke of expensive cigars. I saw a ballroom of sorts peopled with thinkers and drinkers, with mad maestros and shapeshifting beauties. I saw a stage decorated with crimson hearts, the elegant, perforated panels beautifully lit, like the entrance to a French brothel. The richness of reds and purples seemed palpable. I drank it all in—humbled, spellbound, and dying for more.

"What do you think?" came Mr. O.'s voice from above.

He'd been watching my reaction the whole time, clinging to a pillar above, his elongated eyes catching traces of musical light.

Every part of me shook. "I-I-I think… I think…"

"I love you, my friend, but I have to go away, now."

"Wait!"

He had no intention of waiting. He released the pillar and fell backwards into the water, like a man falling into a baptismal pool. I tried to follow his underwater motions, but the railing prevented me from venturing any farther. Moments later he emerged at the far end of the cistern, at the foot of the lighted entrance, where a group of good-humored hooligans dressed in glittering jewels lifted him out of the water and into the tableaux beyond. Passing through, he seemed change color, as if absorbing the light of his world into his skin.

He never turned back to wave goodbye. Just strutted nude into his world as if he owned the place. *What about me?* I thought. Did I not ply him with small comforts over the years? Did I not come to his aid, and see him through his occasional bouts of sickness? What about the scrivener who stashed stories in his drawer at home? Did he not deserve some succor for his earnest attempts at art?

And still the lights dimmed, as the music grew fainter. Deep within came a joyous round of laughter. No party I'd ever attended aspired to the levity seen and heard in the cistern. Oh, I wanted to join them, so much so that jumping into the chop and swimming toward the entrance seemed a small sacrifice, a temporary discomfort.

Giving in to whim, I stood upon the rail and dove in. It seemed like a good idea at the time, but I'd failed to account for the strong current beneath my feet, which flowed, I realized with increasing fear, toward the turbine to my left, the sound it produced while drawing in metric tons of water similar to a Tibetan chant—deep-throated, and whirring like a cyclone. With my feet failing to touch bottom I swam toward the entryway, but halfway there it grew so faint I struggled to discern much detail in the moving images beyond it. The hearts on the lighted stage seemed my only reference point. I tread water as fast as my waterlogged clothes would allow, but by the time I came within ten feet of the wall, I noticed a matrix of mortar appearing between the bricks, then the bricks themselves accrued greater solidity.

I spat, I gasped for air, I fought the current, but by the time I reached the wall, the vision had dwindled to the solemn lumen of a single candle. With a desperate cry, I slapped the wall with both hands, then resumed treading water as the lights went out.

Need I mention the terror I experienced? The only light that remained existed in afterimage behind my eyes—a heart, in fact, snatched in a final glance toward the stage within Mr. O.'s grand ballroom. Everywhere I looked, the heart followed, until it, too, dissipated.

Now, only darkness. Darkness and the taste of foul water on my tongue. I had to rely upon the current drifting past my legs to orient myself back in the direction of the stairs, but releasing the brick seemed a dangerous prospect. Did I have enough energy to make a second swim to safety? The fear of death by drowning does a curious thing to the mind. I'd say you feel like a monkey in the mouth of a lion. In this case, the mouth lay only a few short strokes from where I clung, and if I veered in the wrong direction, down I'd go. To where? A different kind of Hell, I imagined. Or maybe chopped in half, assuming the turbine contained spinning blades, like the whisks of the Model X7 mixer.

Relying upon the same foolhardiness that got me in the water in the first place, I let go the fissures in the bricks, kicked with my legs in the opposite direction, and swam for my life—blind, of course. At any moment I expected something to reach up from the depths and snatch hold of my legs. I paddled faster, and soon found the railing from which I'd leapt. I dragged myself up and over, then crashed to the cement and caught my breath.

All the while the turbine howled, as if angered by my denial of its meal.

Have you ever spent an entire night blind and lost in a sewer system? Have you ever beaten away hungry rats? If you have, then you'll that it ends in a ceaseless cry for help.

And it was by my pathetic pleas that someone opened a sewer lid early the following morning, its single pool of light shining into the darkened waters almost as beautiful as the world beyond the entryway. On the verge of hypothermia, I ascended the ladder and squinted at the solid world above. Everything in its right place. Everything quite ordinary, yet new. Even the rain had vanished. Puffy white clouds drifted overhead. Another kind of Heaven.

I tried to return to the routine of my life, but found it lacking in richness, and somewhat meaningless. One does not stare into another man's dreamland without wanting a similar place to call his own, especially one cursed with a ripe imagination, and who harbors hope for a literary future, no matter how unlikely his prospects of success. Regardless, great secrets must be kept close to the chest. I lied to Monica about how I wound up in the sewer. I told her I'd gone out for a drink (several drinks), and in my inebriated state I slipped down a manhole and belly-flopped in the current, and only by my cat-like reflexes did I survive.

As she wrapped her arms around me, I envisioned Mr. O.'s pantheon of transfigured beauties doing the same, their sweet-scented hair getting caught in my mouth. I lasted less than a month before turning my sights toward Old Dread No. 9. The empty bottles added up—at work, at home—and the deeper I drank, the deeper my vision expanded. And the greater the visions, the greater my ambitions grew. In the doldrums between bottles, I grew morose, and somewhat impossible to live with, according to Monica. She no longer recognized me, and I no longer recognized myself, a change for which I gave thanks, though I noticed my newfound habit had taken a toll on my appearance. I lost interest in food, and a few teeth in the process. Good riddance, thought I, the mad scrivener who hid his personal writing beneath a stack of papers at work, always dibbling and dabbling when my new boss, Jerry Porter, looked away.

My employment at Mills & Berg lasted another year, my marriage two, and with nothing left to lose, except the dwindling respect of my only son, who seemed intent on staying away after completing his studies, I took up residence in the arts district; in fact, in the same studio flat once occupied by Mr. O, although I take greater care of my surroundings, filling it with music and incense, warm light and ambience, though I do still keep his paintings on the wall, if only to remind me of a greater purpose than getting rich off my words.

Besides, what's money? I need time to work, time to dream, time to waste as I please.

I'm now six years strong into my addiction to The Dread, but oh, if six were nine... wouldn't that be sublime? I always told myself I'd complete something important—or at least good—by age fifty, and I feel as though I'm finally breaking through. I feel I'm getting to the heart of things. In fact, I wrote a short piece just this evening that reflects *my* vision of Heaven. Would you like to read it?

Heaven...

Heaven blessed them with a yellow, ash-filled sky. It gave them factories, noise, and slanted, windowless buildings, from which the unrepentant were dragged, then beaten and burned in the street, and made beautiful. It granted them gaping holes, serpentine tongues, and blisters ripe with disease. And the whores were everywhere, dressed in oil, calling out to the tortured and tormented with parted legs, their hair aflame. It gave them dark, urine-drenched alleys, where they emptied themselves into each other without shame, or the need to talk about it afterward. It gave them knife fights in the open market, fountains of sewage, and dusk that never turned to night. It blessed them all, but most of all it blessed the writers, those slouched misfits, who finally had time to get their share while putting it all down on the page, and who would never again lack in fresh material, or wonder if they'd gone too far.

I know what you're thinking: "That doesn't sound like Heaven, Mr. Maxwell." If you're an artist, musician, or painter, or even better, a lover—great lovers are also artists, as a select few can attest—then I'd say you'd better find something else to do, or at least craft a version of Heaven that better suits your sensibilities. After all, each artist must find their own way through the door, and no two paths stretch in the same direction. I believe Mort Gallagher, the banjo player who went missing at the height of his popularity, rode a crest of soundwaves into his dreamworld. Who knows?

In my continued and increasing use of Old Dread No. 9, I've learned more about it. For instance, it's distilled and bottled in France (oui, oui!), and I feel I've come to understand the underlying meaning of its name. What is The Old Dread? The Old Dread is yesterday, yesteryear. It's the creative work you found lacking, and left behind. It's the lackluster life you abandoned in favor of an unpredictable future. It's the promise of a nine-year sabbatical, ending in something beyond your wildest imaginings, assuming you break through the glut of rehashed ideas and old modes of thinking, and paint for yourself a clear picture of your destination, either in words, sound, or pictures, or maybe all three, if you have a touch of DeMille in you. Even if you lack the necessary skills to portray your visions on a tangible medium, you still have the blank canvas of your imagination—an image you can hold and cherish in your dreams.

I must say that it also comes with a few rather serious drawbacks. It takes a tremendous toll on your health, softening you up for a transformation, and you will go mad on occasion. You might curse at passersby. You might spit at the sky. You'll also find the people who once loved you drifting farther away, like stars spiraling outward into cold, dead space. I know this firsthand. In fact, I do get lonely sometimes, as all the time I'd ever wished for I finally have, though these days it yawns in my face. When the hours grow deary, I drink deep and think of my family and friends, all out of contact; all pursuing more practical aims while erasing me from their memories. I wonder if they glance at the obituary section on occasion, peeling back the newsprint, their eyes looking for the letters that comprise the name Tom Maxwell.

No matter. I'm still here. I'm still working.

As for you, I assume you came upon my collection rather by accident, or maybe you found it at the bottom of a pile in some small bookstore, in that dark little corner where they keep the discounted books. In any case, I've included my address in the back. You're welcome to write. Or better yet, stop by. We'll talk about art. Yes! I'll share everything I've learned with you—all the tips and tricks. I'll even let you take a peek at my latest work. Don't ask for a sip of The Dread, though. It's expensive, and I have to ration it. How about a bottle of wine instead? Or whisky. You like whisky, don't you?

What do you say, brother, sister…

…anybody?

Yes, I sure could use a friend.

NOTHING LEFT

When there's nothing left
But spittle on the storyteller's lips
And a circle of fog on the window
Made by his final breath
I'll sit next to him
Inscribe my initials into the dwindling steam
And take his last word
As my own

ABOUT THE AUTHOR

Ken Winkler holds a bachelor's degree in film production from California State University Long Beach, and is the writer and director of the independent horror feature, *Kiss the Abyss*, which received international distribution, including runs on Amazon Prime and other streaming services. He's a five-time Telly Award-winning producer, and has written and produced videos covering a wide range of topics.

Apart from writing fiction, he works as a voiceover artist and plays the drums.

He lives with his wife and rescue animals in La Mirada, California.

CPSIA information can be obtained
at www.ICGtesting.com
Printed in the USA
LVHW040436290123
738059LV00001B/85